Chocolate Swirls and Murder

Holly Holmes Cozy Culinary Mystery - book 2

K.E. O'Connor

K.E. O'Connor Books

CHOCOLATE SWIRLS AND MURDER

Copyright © 2021 K.E. O'Connor.

ISBN: 978-1-9163573-1-0

Written by K.E. O'Connor

Edited by Amy Hart

Cover design by Stunning Book Covers

Beta read by my wonderful early review team. You're all amazing.

Chapter 1

"Say you'll take part in the food fair baking contest." Princess Alice Audley strolled around the kitchen behind me as I prepared a tray of triple chocolate cupcakes for hungry café visitors.

"I'm too busy to consider the contest." I twirled chocolate icing over the cupcakes and passed them to Louise to go out to the café.

"You have a flair for making cakes look beautiful. I always tell people your food is a work of art." Alice had been buzzing around me like a cute, mildly annoying fly for ten minutes.

"Delicious works of art, I hope." I adjusted my grip on the tray of warm cinnamon buns I'd pulled out of the oven before placing it on the counter to cool.

Alice fluttered her naturally long dark lashes. "I'll be your best friend if you enter the contest."

I chuckled. Despite moving in radically different social circles, I considered Alice a really good friend. "Tourist season is in full swing. Chef Heston won't let me have the time off to prepare. And you know how fierce the competition will be. I'd have to bring my A game. No slacking off allowed."

"I'll order him to give you the time off." Alice jammed her hands on her hips and flipped her blonde hair over one shoulder with a toss of her head. "The public deserve to see how beautiful your cakes are. Plus, how delicious they are." She grabbed a cinnamon bun from the tray. "Ouch! That's hot."

I arched an eyebrow. "Ovens tend to do that to food. Leave them for a while. They won't be ready to ice for another half an hour, at least. And the frosting always brings out the cinnamon."

She pouted. "I want cake, and I want it now."

"Yes, your majesty." I dipped a quick curtsey before walking to the chiller cabinet. I took out a batch of fresh cream horns dipped in Belgian chocolate. "Have one of these."

"You see!" She held up the flaky pastry horn. "Perfection."

"Eat that and stop bothering me about the baking contest."

"But you'll be a huge success. Take some space on the Audley Castle stand on the day. You can sell your cupcakes to see how much people love your desserts," Alice said. "That will liven things up. We only ever have boring information on there about our castle and my dusty old ancestors. That's yawn city for most people. However, if you entice them with luscious treats they can buy, you'll see how popular you are. Then you'll want to enter the contest."

Every year, Audley Castle held a fantastic food fair. Vendors came from all over the country to sell delicious treats to visitors. It had been running for over fifty years. This year, there was a full day of selling, followed by three days of competition, with the best bakers and cooks fighting it out with perfect pies and cakes to win in different categories, plus, an overall grand winner.

"Holly Holmes! I insist upon it." Alice wagged a finger at me. "You know what I do to people who don't follow my orders."

"Threaten to chop off their heads?" Sometimes, those threats sounded a bit too real.

A peal of laughter shot out of her mouth. "That's right. You can't deprive the world of your treats. The Duke and Duchess are even judging this year."

"It doesn't feel right that I enter," I said. "I work here."

"That doesn't disqualify you from entering," Alice said. "I've checked the rules. Besides, it's all judged fairly. Please say you'll enter."

"Maybe next year."

"Chef Heston!" Alice hurried over as my grumpy boss entered the kitchen and grabbed hold of his arm, dragging him toward me. "You have to tell Holly to help on the castle stand at the food fair and enter the competition. She must take part."

"Must she now." His dark eyes narrowed as he glared at me. "Trying to get out of work again, Holmes?"

I lifted my hands and shook my head. "I've already told Princess Alice that I'm too busy in the kitchen."

"And I've told her it's her civic duty to share her treats with everyone," Alice said. "There's plenty of room on the Audley Castle display stand. And we're short of people to look after it. This is the perfect solution. Holly can do a few hours and sell delicious treats. She can also send people to the café, so it's a win-win all round."

Some people thought Alice was nothing but an extremely beautiful face surrounded by a mass of dazzling blonde curls. She was nothing short of a genius when she wanted to be.

Chef Heston grunted. "We'll be busy during the food fair. People still come to the café, especially if they've been looking around for several hours and need somewhere to sit."

"You can spare Holly," Alice said. "Look at all the cakes she's already baked today. And you've got a whole team working here. You won't miss her."

I gritted my teeth. I sort of hoped he would, or he might decide I was superfluous to requirements and get rid of me.

"Will you promote the café if you do this?" he asked me.

"Of course," I said. "I can put out samples of what we have at the café. And I'll sell our cakes as well."

"And you must get her to take part in the competition," Alice said.

"Hmmm. I'm not sure about that. That will take her away from her duties," Chef Heston said.

"Don't be such a meanie!" Alice swatted his arm.

I masked a smile behind my hand. Only a princess could get away with doing that. "I don't mind not being a part of the competition." Although if I did enter, I might test out a Neapolitan and red velvet layer cake with a chocolate chip mousse.

"You do have those unusual flourishes you add to your creations," Chef Heston said. "It would be interesting to see what other people thought of them."

"That's a yes!" Alice stood on her tiptoes and kissed Chef Heston's cheek.

He flushed bright pink before turning and hurrying away.

"I'll pay for that," I said. "You bullied him into getting me involved."

Alice's eyes glittered as she beamed at me. "So, what are you going to bake?"

I grinned back, enthused by her excitement. "Well, I was thinking of—"

The kitchen door opened. Lord Rupert Audley bumbled in, smiling when he saw me. "I was hoping you might have some of your triple chocolate fudge brownies available. I've been thinking about them all morning. In fact, I had a dream about one last night."

"Some came out of the oven ten minutes ago," I said. "They're still warm."

Rupert pushed his messy blond hair out of his face. "They're perfect like that. Not that they aren't delicious at any other time. You always bake perfection."

"You can't beat a just out of the oven brownie." I plated one up and handed it over.

"I'm glad you're here." Alice bit into her cream horn. "I'm twisting Holly's arm to get her involved in the cake contest. She's pretending she doesn't have enough time. I know you can convince her otherwise."

"Well, you do make jolly delicious cakes," he said. "If I had a vote, I'd vote for you to win the whole thing."

My cheeks grew warm, and I looked away. "That's kind of you. However, as I was explaining to your sister—"

"Stuff and nonsense," Alice said. "Besides, it's too late. I've put your name down."

"You've done what?" I stared at her in disbelief.

She grinned and ate more cream horn. "It's all arranged."

"What if I'd said no?"

"I knew you wouldn't." Alice giggled.

I bit my bottom lip. I was secretly excited about being a part of this contest. I had four main loves in my life: my adorable corgi cross, Meatball, who was currently lounging in his kennel outside the kitchen; my interest in history; my love of new fitness trends; and baking. It wasn't so long ago that I ran my own café. It didn't end well, but I loved nothing more than starting the day with my head full of recipes to tempt people with.

Chef Heston returned and loudly cleared his throat. "This is a kitchen I'm trying to run here, not a social event."

Alice giggled again before grabbing her brother's arm. "We're going." She winked at me before they left the kitchen.

Chef Heston shook his head. "There's a delivery you need to do."

"Where to?" I asked.

"Mrs. Brown."

"Is the van free?"

He smirked. "Take the bike. The exercise will do you good. I noticed you've been sampling your own brownies again."

My eyes widened. "Taste testing is an important part of the job."

He snorted a laugh. "The bike's outside waiting for you."

I repressed a sigh as I took off my apron and headed outside with the four boxes of cakes for Mrs. Brown. Chef Heston loved to torture me by insisting I ride the delivery bike into Audley St. Mary.

Not that it was a huge chore, unless the trolley really was loaded with cake. But Audley St. Mary had a few hills, and I always ended up puffed out and sweaty by the time my deliveries were over.

I hadn't had time to take Meatball for a walk at lunchtime, we'd been so rushed with orders, so once the cakes were secured on the trolley, I hurried around to his kennel.

He bounced up as soon as he saw me and wagged his little brown tail. He was my best friend, and it had been a condition of me taking this job that I could bring him with me. And, although quite rightly, Meatball wasn't allowed in the kitchen, I'd been given permission to erect a luxurious kennel right outside the door so I could keep an eye on him while I worked.

"Come on, boy," I said. "Delivery time."

"Woof woof." That was his version of saying yes. He waited patiently as I attached his harness and helmet—safety first—before lifting him into the wicker basket secured on the front of the bike.

Yes, it was that kind of bike. Old-fashioned, heavy-framed, and with no gears. It was part of the image Audley Castle portrayed. We had a lot of traditions at the castle and apparently using bikes with no gears was one of them.

I headed away from the castle and made my way up and down the first hill. By the time I'd reached Mrs. Brown's thirty minutes later, I was out of breath and my legs felt like they'd gotten a workout.

I climbed off the bike, lifting a hand in greeting as several residents wandered past.

Audley St. Mary was a small, friendly village. The village had grown up around Audley Castle and was proud to have mostly independent stores and a wonderful history that dated back hundreds of years.

I petted Meatball on the back before untying the cake boxes and walking along the pretty cottage garden pathway to Mrs. Brown's front door.

She lived in a tiny thatched cottage on the edge of the village. As far as I knew, she lived alone, and rumor had it she had more money than the Queen.

I knocked at the door.

Mrs. Brown's wrinkled face lit up as she opened it and saw the cakes. "Holly! You're my savior. When I contacted the kitchen yesterday to put in my last-minute request, I wasn't sure you'd have time for me." She gestured me into the cottage.

"We've always got time for you, Mrs. Brown."

She smiled. "I'd forgotten all about the supper gathering I'm hosting this evening. My eight friends and I have been getting together for almost fifty years. Once a month, we take turns to host a small party. It must be my age making me forget. I only remembered because I was chatting to Dorothy on the phone last night and she said 'see you tomorrow'. I pretended that I knew what she meant. It was only when I consulted my diary that it came flooding back. Never get old, Holly." She patted my hand.

I wouldn't mind being as sprightly as Mrs. Brown when I was in my eighties. She was independent, got out of her cottage several times a week, and I'd even seen her at the village Pilates class.

I set the cakes on the wooden kitchen counter. "These should ensure the party gets off to a good start."

"Absolutely. Let's take a peek." She lifted a box lid and sighed in delight. "Your cakes are so pretty. I always know when you've baked them. Look at those tiny flowers on the top. They're so beautiful, I feel guilty eating them."

I chuckled, pleased she'd noticed my careful eye for detail. "Please do eat them. I'd be offended if you didn't."

"Oh! Of course. It'll be my pleasure. We plan to eat every last one. Although I did order an extra box so I could enjoy some later in the week." She closed the box lid and studied me in silence for a few seconds. "Do you see anything of Lady Philippa while you're at the castle?"

"Of course. She's got a sweet tooth and is often asking for cakes to be sent to her room. I sometimes take them if we're busy in the kitchen."

"Oh! Is she unwell? She can't leave her bedroom?" Mrs. Brown's age-spotted hand fluttered against her narrow chest.

"No, nothing like that. She tends to spend most of her time in the east turret. She likes it up there. It's got a good view of the grounds." I deliberately didn't mention that

Lady Philippa believed her family kept her locked in there. "Do you know her?"

Mrs. Brown looked out the window. "We used to be friends. Every time I have one of these gatherings, I wonder if I should rekindle our friendship."

"Did you have a falling out?"

She looked back at me and her gaze hardened. "I should say. At one of our tea parties, she declared that somebody was about to die. I was mortified. How can you have a fun party when someone just declared a death is about to occur?"

My eyes widened. It wasn't the first time I'd heard about Lady Philippa's ability to predict the future, especially when it came to somebody's demise. "Did the person die?"

"Yes! That's the worst thing. Because of her unfortunate ability, it was set in stone."

"Her ... ability?"

"Oh yes! And you must have heard that the Audleys, and those who marry into the family, become cursed," Mrs. Brown said. "A love curse so I've heard. The rumors are only fueled by the fact they live in a haunted castle."

"I don't know about ghosts." I'd experienced my fair share of spooky noises and cold spots but wasn't ready to admit there might be ghosts in the place I worked. "It can get a bit drafty in there, though."

"Drafty!" Mrs. Brown shook her head. "You'd be wise to keep an open mind. Lady Philippa and that whole family have mystery surrounding them. No, I think it's better if I keep my distance. If I invite her to another party, she'll only do something dramatic. That would be the end of my social life."

"Yes, I suppose it might. Well, I'd better get going," I said, not sure I was in a position to advise on such a delicate matter. "Busy day at the castle. Lots of baking to do."

"Of course." Mrs. Brown led me back to the door, tucking a ten pound note in my hand as she did so. "Buy yourself something nice."

"Thanks." I smiled and nodded. The tips were amazing from the wealthy villagers. They all went into my fund to buy new recipe books and go on cooking courses.

"And it's the food fair soon. I trust you'll be taking part."

"I wasn't until about an hour ago. I'll be on the Audley Castle stand if you want to drop by."

"With free samples?" She opened the door, a hopeful glint in her eyes.

"Of course." I smiled and waved goodbye as I headed back to the bike. Everyone seemed to know about the curses and hauntings at the castle. It wasn't such a surprise. The tourist brochure and the website played up to the fact the place was supposed to be haunted. And I'd experienced first-hand how spookily accurate Lady Philippa's predictions could be.

I unclipped Meatball's helmet and took him for a fifteen-minute walk around the village green before we headed back and I grabbed the bike. I turned it toward Audley Castle and cycled back as fast as I could.

I had a lot of work to do if I was entering this cake competition. Bakers could be a competitive bunch as we tried to outdo each other with the lightest sponge and sweetest buttercream. I needed to get testing and baking if I was to stand a chance of winning.

I'd only just settled Meatball back in his kennel and walked into the kitchen to wash up when Chef Heston caught me.

"You're late."

"I took the delivery to Mrs. Brown, and she wanted to chat. It would have been rude not spend a few minutes with a lonely old lady."

"Sure it would." He scowled at me. "Lady Philippa has been asking for you. Take this up to her rooms immediately." He handed me a tea tray with a pink flowered teapot, china tea cups, and four strawberry scones with clotted cream and strawberry preserves.

"I'll get right on that." I gulped down my sudden nerves. The east turret was never my favorite place.

Mrs. Brown's comments about the castle being haunted were front and center of my mind as I walked through my first cold spot. It was nothing. This was an ancient castle, built in Jacobean times. Cracks would appear over the years and the cold would get in. That's all it was.

I shoved away my fears and dashed up the spiral staircase to the east turret rooms.

"Holly Holmes! Where have you been?" Lady Philippa spoke before she could even see me as I hurried past the large leaded windows toward her lounge.

"Sorry I'm late. I got here as quickly as I could." I nudged the door open with my hip and entered the room. It was an opulent living space, with expensive velvet curtains draped around the windows, red silk wallpaper, and luxurious designer furniture scattered around the room. Lady Philippa also had a huge bedroom with an ornate four poster bed. I had no idea how they'd gotten it up the spiral staircase. Maybe it had been built in place.

"You've been on my mind." Lady Philippa gestured to a side table by the high-backed chair she sat in. "Pour me a cup of tea. I'm parched."

"Of course. Why have you been thinking about me?"

"Because of who you've been to visit." She was dressed in a demure beige silk dress, diamonds glittering around her neck. "You've been gossiping about me."

I looked up hurriedly as I handed her a tea cup. "I wouldn't say gossiping." How did she know Mrs. Brown had been discussing her less than two hours ago?

"My gut never lies," she said. "And I smell lavender. Olivia Brown always wore a lavender perfume."

My mouth dropped open.

"Stop trying to catch flies, girl. Sit down and sort those scones. Remember, I like my preserves under my cream."

I snapped my mouth shut and dealt with the scones before handing her two on a plate.

"The rest are for you," she said. "I imagine you've worked up an appetite cycling to the village and back with those cakes for Olivia and her gaggle of wrinkled old girlfriends."

I glanced at the binoculars on the window ledge and smiled. "Have you been busy birdwatching again?"

She grinned. "I'm a keen birdwatcher. There's always something fascinating outside to keep me occupied. So, what has Olivia been gossiping about?"

"Nothing bad about you. She was saying that she knew you, and you used to go to her parties."

Her grin faded, and she nodded. "We used to be close. She was a real firecracker. All the men fell in love when they saw Olivia and those raven curls."

"She's not raven haired anymore," I said.

Lady Philippa patted her professionally dyed and styled bobbed hair. "None of us are the same as we used to be. How is she?"

"Doing well from what I can tell," I said.

"She still has that little cottage?"

"That's right." I bit into my scone. The perfect combination of cream and sweet strawberry preserves made me sigh in pleasure.

"She never married. Back in our heyday, marriages were often arranged, especially in the upper classes. It helped cement relationships and forge business deals. I can't think of anything worse. Olivia got several proposals of marriage, and her family tried to set her up on numerous occasions, but she comes from a moneyed background and inherited the lot when her parents died. She never found anyone to love. Good for her, living a life she always wanted without being saddled with some weak-chinned wonder who'd bore her to death."

"She might miss you," I said cautiously. "She was interested in how you were doing."

Lady Philippa gave a most unladylike snort. "I doubt that very much. Did she tell you why I stopped going to her parties?"

"Something about predicting a death?"

"Exactly! She shunned me for telling the truth." She shook her head. "One second, we were all laughing and joking, then I announced my prediction and it all went wrong. Olivia said she was feeling unwell and everyone had to leave. The next week, I wandered past her cottage and they were all together. Olivia didn't invite me back after that."

"Maybe it's time to mend that bridge," I said. "It could be fun to host a few parties here for your friends."

She waved a hand in the air as if to dismiss the idea. "Too much has happened since then. It would be like strangers meeting. We'd have nothing to say to each other."

"True friendship isn't like that. I have friends I only see once a year, but it's like we've never been apart. We just pick up a conversation and off we go."

"Hmmm. Lucky you."

"Don't you get lonely up in this turret on your own?"

"If my family didn't keep me locked up here, I'd be free to make new friends," she said with a dramatic sigh. "Anyway, I didn't call you up here to gossip about my former friends. I want to talk about the death I see in the very near future."

Chapter 2

"You see a death occurring?" I gulped. "I hope it's not mine."

Lady Philippa tipped her head back and laughed. "You're going to live a very long time, Holly Holmes. But I've had the same dream three nights in a row. It never ends well."

"What does your dream show you?"

"I've struggled to understand this one, which is why I'm only just mentioning it. Sometimes, my visions can be tricky. I've been dreaming about a pig."

"Is the pig doing anything in particular? Does the pig have a gun and is aiming it at someone?"

She narrowed her eyes. "Of course not. How can a pig hold a gun in his trotters?"

I pressed my lips together to stop from smiling. "Excellent point. So, what's the pig doing?"

"He's a handsome fellow. A big pink porker. He's wearing a curly wig."

"A pig in a wig. And he used his wig to do something bad? Did he stuff it in someone's mouth and suffocate them?"

She tutted. "I won't tell you the rest of my prediction if you keep on with that nonsense."

I lifted a hand and settled back in my seat. "I won't say another word. Tell me your whole dream. Maybe we can figure it out."

Lady Philippa pursed her lips. "Very well. My wig-wearing pig is dining on a bowl of figs."

My eyebrows shot up. "A pig in a wig eating figs. This could be a poem, not a portent of death."

"You can make it into what you like, but those three things are linked. I won't get a good night of sleep until this is resolved. Not that I sleep much these days, anyway. Whatever that pig has planned, he needs to do it quickly and stop bothering me."

"Maybe these dreams aren't connected to the pig doing anything wrong. Perhaps this is connected to the food fair. It always causes disruption at the castle. We've been taking deliveries in the kitchen for two weeks. Chef Heston is almost tearing his hair out. Hey! Maybe that's what you've seen. Chef Heston gets so stressed that his hair falls out, and he needs to wear a wig."

"This has nothing to do with that grumpy chef. And I've been around for all the food fairs. I love welcoming people into our grounds."

"Could it be your subconscious telling you that you want to go to the food fair? I bet there'll be all kinds of tasty treats. Probably plenty of pig and fig themed items to sample."

Her blue eyes sparkled. "I'd love to visit the food fair. If only I wasn't locked in this turret, I'd be there all day."

I opened my mouth to protest. The door to her room was always open whenever I came by. Instead, I simply nodded. "I'm going to be there this year."

Lady Philippa smiled warmly. "I predicted that as well. If you weren't at that fair displaying your fabulous food, it would be a crime. What will you showcase?"

"Mostly things we're already preparing in the kitchen," I said. "Princess Alice talked me into it, and she twisted Chef Heston's arm to agree to me being involved. I'll be on the Audley Castle stand."

"I expect to see you entering the cake competition as well. You'll give all those show-offs who think their food is the best, a run for their money."

"Do you predict a win in my future?"

Lady Philippa closed her eyes and swayed in her seat. "Oh dear!"

I gasped and leaned forward. "What do you see? Don't tell me the judges hate my cake."

"I see bad times ahead for you. Be careful at the food fair."

"You don't think the pig is coming for me? He's not going to eat my cake?"

"This problem is much closer to home. Be careful of who you let near your cake."

"Someone might sabotage it? One of the other contestants gets vicious?"

She opened her eyes. "I cannot tell you. My predictions are rarely that specific."

"Of course. That would make life too easy if you could tell me exactly who I needed to avoid and who might die."

"Cheeky young thing! Just keep your eyes open and you'll figure it out."

"A pig in a wig eating figs." I nodded sagely. "Got it."

She tapped me on the knee. "Don't expect to see a jolly porker strutting around wearing a fine wig while he munches on a bowl of figs. Think in the abstract."

"Of course, the abstract. That makes it simple."

Lady Philippa chuckled. "And I expect you to bring me plenty of treats from the fair. I'll watch through my binoculars, so I'll know if you miss anything out."

"I promise, I'll make up a special tray for you. You won't miss a thing."

She nodded, seeming content with that answer. "Now, off you go. Chef Heston will be shouting if you don't hurry."

I grinned as I stood and headed for the door. "Even I could make that prediction." I dashed down the spiral stone staircase and back to the kitchen.

I couldn't figure out her prediction. Maybe Lady Philippa was having a bad day. We all had strange dreams. I once dreamed I was living on a space station surrounded by lonely aliens looking for love. It didn't end well. I never could develop a taste for tentacles.

I tensed as I spotted Campbell Milligan on duty, the ever-watchful head of private security for the Audleys. He stood with his back erect and his hands behind him. He was clearly on duty, so I ignored him.

Ever since he'd had me arrested for murder, I was cautious around Campbell. We'd cleared the air, but he was a man driven by logic and evidence. I tended to follow my gut and perhaps paid too much attention to Lady Philippa's predictions. The two of us would never see eye to eye.

My head twisted at the sound of barking. That was Meatball. I'd recognize his throaty rumble anywhere.

"Woof woof woof woof woof." Whatever was going on, he was excited, and he was heading straight toward me.

A high-pitched yip followed straight after his barks. A petite, fluffy ginger corgi sped around the corner, her tail up and her dark eyes glittering as she bounded along the corridor and straight past me.

A few seconds later, Meatball careened around the same corner, his little legs a blur as he chased after the new arrival.

"Hold it right there, buddy." I tried to block him, but he dodged around me with a happy woof.

I turned and stared at him in surprise. Meatball rarely disobeyed me. He must have seen something he liked in this new corgi.

The corgi slowed and looked over her shoulder, bouncing on her paws as Meatball drew nearer. She let him get within sniffing distance before yipping again and racing away, heading straight toward Campbell.

"Oh no you don't," I muttered under my breath. The last thing I needed was Meatball getting me in trouble with Campbell.

I raced after the dogs, determined to grab Meatball before he caused trouble.

I grimaced as the dogs shot past Campbell. He didn't so much as flinch.

"Hey! Stop those dogs," I yelled as I raced after them.

"Having trouble with your corgis?" Campbell asked.

"You could say that." I slowed as I reached him and looked around. The dogs had vanished. "Where did they go?"

The trace of a smile flickered at the edge of his mouth.

"Come on! Help a girl out. You must have seen which direction they went," I said.

"Your dog shouldn't run around loose in the castle," Campbell muttered.

"I have no idea how he got in. You know he's got his kennel outside. He should be in there." I looked along the corridor.

"Try the doggy door."

I stared up at Campbell. And I mean, I had to really stare up. He had a good foot and a few inches in height on me and stood an impressive six feet five inches. "What are you talking about?"

"You don't know about the doggy doors in the castle?"

"No! Why don't you show me?"

"The Duchess had them installed," Campbell said. "Not this duchess, the one before her. Go to the left-hand side of that door over there, duck down, and you'll find what you're looking for."

I glared at him. "This had better not be a joke."

"You know me. I never joke."

That was true. I hurried to the door and ducked. At first, I didn't see anything, but as I ran my hand along the wall, it moved. A small tunnel looked like it had been cut through the thick stone wall and a dog-sized wooden door added. That was where my missing dog must have gone.

I stood and grabbed the handle of the main door. Campbell's large hand clamped on my shoulder.

"Going somewhere?" he asked.

"To get my dog back."

"These are the family's private quarters."

"Then you'd better escort me in," I said. "I have to make sure Meatball doesn't get in trouble. He seemed keen on that corgi. I've not seen her before."

"The Duchess acquired her a week ago. She's been with the vet and then at the doggy parlor."

"Have you been overseeing that important task? I bet you got trained for just that sort of thing when you worked for the government."

He leaned closer. "I trained for many things, including how to get rid of irritating problems."

I swallowed. As hard as I tried, Campbell intimidated me. "Good to know. So, are we going in?"

He dropped his hold on me and nodded. He lifted his arm and spoke into the sleeve. "Alpha two, this is Alpha one. I'm on the move. Entering the Canopy Room. My position will be unguarded, over."

"Copy that, Alpha one. We'll move position to ensure all routes are covered, over."

"Received. Out." Campbell lowered his arm.

I looked at his sleeve. I couldn't see anything that could be used as a communication device. "How does that work? Have you got a mic wired up your sleeve? Why not use the doodlebug thing in your ear?"

A muscle in his jaw twitched. "The doodlebug thing is on the fritz."

"Or you could keep a phone in your pocket. That would work. And I've always been a fan of walkie talkies. Do you use those to speak to your teams?"

"You ask too many questions."

"I'm curious. Wouldn't it be easier to have something in your pocket?"

"What makes you think I don't?"

I pursed my lips. "You have backups for everything."

He opened the door. "Shall we?"

I bit back a retort and hurried into the room. I'd only seen a fraction of the family's private quarters. They kept a dozen rooms exclusively for use as a family, plus the bedrooms. The public never got access to them. Not so much as a peek.

This was the first time I'd seen the Canopy Room. I stared open-mouthed in amazement. The room was awash with green interlaced with gold. There were gold mirrors, gold cushions, and green and gold silk wallpaper.

Campbell nudged me not too gently with his elbow. "Quit staring and find your dog before he pees on something he shouldn't."

"Give me a minute. This might be the only time I ever see this room. It's beautiful."

"You've had your minute. Move it. And if I find your dog has done his business in this room—"

"Meatball's well-trained. He'd never go to the toilet in somewhere as stunning as this."

"He can't be that well-trained. He ignored you when you tried to bring him to heel."

I glowered at Campbell. "He was just … excited. He'd seen a beautiful woman and wanted to get to know her better. You must know what that's like. Have you been on any good dates recently?"

Campbell snorted. "My private life is just that."

"Your everything life is just that. You should loosen up, make a few friends, take a night off. It's fun to have a social life."

"What's your social life like?"

"Oh! Well … I'm busy at work. There are always cakes to bake." My private life was dire. I had friends in the village but was still finding my feet after moving here just over a year ago. And as for going on dates with eligible bachelors, that hadn't happened for a long time.

"Maybe sort out your own private life before you nose into mine," Campbell said.

I grumbled under my breath as I hurried away to find Meatball. I'd been called nosy once or twice, but it was good to have a healthy curiosity.

And I was curious now, walking past these beautiful antiques. "I'd be too scared to use any of this. What if you break something in here?"

"If you broke anything, your feet wouldn't touch the ground. You'd be arrested," Campbell said, following me like a second shadow.

"Come off it," I said. "Accidents happen."

"Not on my watch." He gestured me to keep walking. "Don't touch anything."

"Ooooh! This looks like it's from the Ming Dynasty." I stared at the tall vase decorated with robed figures surrounded by forest.

"What do you know about the Ming Dynasty?"

"I studied it at university," I said. "I did a history degree."

"How did that work out for you?"

I wrinkled my nose. "Not brilliant. The only career option offered to me when I graduated was a history teacher, and I didn't want that. Instead, I find myself living among history every day in this castle. And I've never lost my love for the Tudor period. There's something exciting about that part of our history. Don't you agree?"

He grunted. "Fascinating."

I shrugged. Campbell clearly wasn't a lover of history.

Meatball and the new corgi darted out from under a chaise lounge and raced toward us.

"Grab them!" I ducked and held my arms out to Meatball.

He swerved past me at the last second and doubled back. The cute corgi was now chasing him, and she was having a great time.

"Huh! He's fast for a little dog," Campbell said.

"When he wants something, he can be determined." I hurried after the corgis.

"It's in their nature." Campbell walked beside me.

"You know about corgis?"

"I do. The Duchess takes them everywhere. I've gotten to know her pets over the years."

"And you like them?"

"I don't dislike them. Although they can be stubborn little critters."

I grinned. "Meatball has been known to be bull-headed."

"Reminds me of his owner."

"Here they come," I said. "You head off the female. I'll grab Meatball. He might not respond too well if you go for him."

Campbell smirked. "One little dog won't trouble me."

Maybe he didn't know his corgis as well as he thought. Their determination when they wanted something was second to none. I'd seen it in Meatball when he set his eyes on a particularly delicious sandwich I'd made. If I didn't watch it like a hawk, it would be gone in a flash.

"Here we go. Get ready." I focused on Meatball. His tail was up and he almost skipped with joy.

The corgis owned by the Duchess were downright mean to him, so he must have been delighted at finding a friend. I felt a bit mean for breaking up the party.

"Get ready," I repeated.

"I was born ready," Campbell muttered.

I chuckled at the cliché as he crouched and flexed his fingers. He looked like he was about to go into a rugby scrum, not stop a corgi in her tracks.

"Meatball!" I patted my thighs. "Come here, boy. I've got liver sausage in my pocket. You love liver sausage. Come get a tasty treat."

His ears pricked at the word treat and he slowed, glancing at me.

"That's it, boy. All-you-can-eat doggy buffet if only you come here."

"He's not thinking with his head," Campbell said.

"That happens to a lot of guys," I said.

Campbell snorted again.

Meatball slowed to a trot, but the female corgi kept charging along, her excitement up.

Campbell lunged at the corgi at the same time as I grabbed Meatball. I scooped him into my arms and hoisted his front paws over my shoulder, clamping his back legs securely in my other hand so he wouldn't escape.

"Hey, handsome boy. Have you been making friends? How did you get in the castle?"

"Woof woof," he barked happily, giving my cheek a quick lick, his gaze still on the other corgi.

I turned and just about managed to stop from bursting out with laughter. Campbell was sprawled on the floor as the dog danced away from him.

"Having a spot of bother with your corgi?" I grinned as I walked over with Meatball, feeling more than a bit smug at capturing my prey.

Campbell climbed smoothly to his feet and scowled. "She dodged at the last second. I wasn't expecting it."

"Corgis are smart."

"She's not getting away." He stalked after the corgi, weaving around the expensive furniture as she ducked and dived to avoid Campbell.

"You're scaring her," I said. "And you don't want her to damage anything. She'll be arrested."

"That rule only applies to humans," Campbell said. "The corgis can get away with murder."

My thoughts briefly turned to what Lady Philippa had said. She hadn't told me if the death would be from natural causes or if somebody was out to harm another person. I should have clarified that, but perhaps her pig in his wig didn't mention it in her dream state. He must have been too busy eating from that bowl of figs to worry about little details like that.

I shook my head. It was most likely a lurid dream. Lady Philippa had gotten carried away with the excitement of the upcoming food fair.

"Got you!" Campbell dived, grabbed the dog, and did a forward roll as he tucked the corgi against his chest, coming to stand upright with the surprised looking dog in his arms.

"Wow! I'm impressed. Did they teach you that move in spy school?"

The corner of his mouth curled up. "Dog napping is a key part of my skills. Have you got yours under control?"

"Always," I said.

"It looked like it while he was scampering along the corridors of the castle ignoring you."

"It's good that my dog's independent." I lifted my chin.

"Stubborn dog, stubborn owner," Campbell muttered.

The door to the Canopy Room opened. I froze as Duke Henry Audley and Duchess Isabella Audley walked in.

"Goodness! I didn't know we had guests." The Duchess walked over, a smile on her face as she spotted the corgi. "I've been looking for Priscilla. You naughty girl, you got away from me."

"I was just returning her to you." Campbell swiftly handed the dog to the Duchess.

"Thank you, Campbell. You're always looking out for my dogs." The Duchess's attention turned to me. "And you have a corgi too. I've heard about the legendary Meatball."

"He's taken a shine to your new dog," I said.

"Oh, how adorable." The Duchess walked over and petted Meatball's head.

He wagged his tail and sniffed her hand before giving it a lick.

"And what a handsome boy," she said. "He's not a purebred, is he?"

"No, Meatball's a mixture. There's definitely some terrier in there."

"He's charming. I'm sure Priscilla will be thrilled to have a new friend if you think they'll get along."

"Of course. I think he's in love."

The Duchess laughed softly. "I'm introducing Priscilla to the others slowly. They can be a bit ... feisty when a new arrival comes along. It takes them a while to organize the pack order, but I couldn't resist this adorable face." She kissed the top of the dog's head.

Her pack of corgis were difficult. They always enjoyed chasing and picking on Meatball every chance they got.

"We should organize a doggy play date," the Duchess said. "What do you think, my dear?" She gestured to the Duke, who'd been peering at an oil painting on the wall ever since he'd entered the room.

"Oh, yes. Very good. Whatever you think. We can get one of the boys to sort the dogs out."

I tilted my head. What did he mean by that?

"My love, we don't have boys. Holly here owns Meatball, and Sammy walks my dogs when I don't have the time."

"That's right, I always forget," the Duke said. "And the servants will be busy with the food fair soon enough."

"Staff, not servants, my angel." The Duchess lifted an eyebrow, an amused smile on her face. "My husband prefers the old days." She lowered her voice. "He sometimes forgets that we don't live in the nineteenth century."

"I love history," I said. "I understand why the Duke is so fascinated by that time period."

Campbell discreetly cleared his throat.

I imagined him glaring at me for being so forward, but the Duchess had started the conversation. It would be rude not to take part.

"Don't get him talking about the family history," the Duchess said quietly. "He'll never let you leave."

I nodded. "We should go. This is your private room, but Meatball chased after Priscilla and—"

"Don't think anything of it. I'm sure Campbell had everything in hand." The Duchess nodded at him. "He's my top bodyguard."

"He's very good at catching dogs," I said, trying hard to keep a neutral expression on my face.

She grinned. "That he is. I've had him racing after my cherubs on numerous occasions. Come on, my dear. Let's get you settled in your chair with a book."

"Ah. Yes. Very good," the Duke said.

"Oh, will we see you at the food fair, Holly?" the Duchess asked as she reached a set of antique high-back chairs with gold arms. "I'm looking forward to your entry in the cake competition. We're judging this year."

"I'll be there," I said, pleased she remembered my desserts. "I'll try not to let you down."

"Your food could never let us down. You're a genius with your cakes. I can't wait to sample them." She nodded before turning and walking to the bookcase, her husband trailing along behind her.

"You need to leave." Campbell was right behind me, his voice low and slightly menacing in my ear.

I turned and stepped away. "I wish you wouldn't creep up on me like that."

"Then stop poking around in places you shouldn't."

I longed to argue with him, but not when the Duke and Duchess were present. "I'm going. I've got cakes to deal with."

"And a dog." Campbell briefly petted Meatball before he strode out of the room.

Meatball whined and looked longingly at Priscilla.

"Sorry, buddy. She's way out of your league. We're not meant for royalty. Come on, let's go get you that liver sausage I promised you."

Chapter 3

"What do you think of this one?" I passed a small slice of dark chocolate and rosewater sponge cake to Alice.

She took a bite and closed her eyes as she chewed carefully. "As with all the others you've fed me in the last hour, it's scrumptious. I don't know how you'll decide which one to enter in the competition."

I scratched my chin. Neither did I. I'd baked a chocolate and orange sponge, but that didn't seem elaborate enough. I'd also tried a twist on chocolate eclairs, filling them with a gooey chocolate caramel and topping them with spun sugar, but they didn't look quite right. Then I'd stuck to a classic Victoria sponge filled with strawberry preserves and buttercream. And that was just in the last two hours. There were several more discarded experiments on the counter.

I needed something that would stand out without looking ostentatious. Audley Castle was built on firm and ancient traditions. The judges wouldn't like anything too artsy or new-fangled. It had to be something traditional, look amazing, and taste great.

"I really can't decide," Alice said. "We need a second opinion."

"Who do you have in mind?" I asked.

"I've got just the person. He always tells it like it is, and has a sweet tooth, although he tries to hide it." She grinned as she climbed off the stool by the kitchen counter and left the room.

Who could she be talking about? If she brought in Rupert, he'd be no good. He loved everything I baked. Even if I made a cake mix from a packet and simply added an egg and some milk, he'd say it was the best thing I'd ever baked.

The kitchen door opened. Alice was dragging behind her a reluctant looking Campbell.

I hadn't seen him since the corgi wrangling incident in the Canopy Room two days ago.

"This is your perfect taste tester," Alice said.

"I'm on duty, Princess," he said. "I can't be distracted."

"You're guarding me. You can hardly do that effectively by lurking outside the kitchen door. In here, you'll see if any danger is sneaking up on me."

Campbell looked at the selection of cakes on the counter, and his eyes gleamed. "Perhaps you're right."

"I always am," Alice said. "Try this ... what was it, Holly?" She pointed at the cake she'd just sampled.

"Belgian chocolate sponge with ganache chocolate icing and rosewater. I'm trying a twist on an old tradition." I offered a piece to Campbell.

He took a bite and chewed. "Not bad. The sponge is a bit dense."

"My sponge is never dense!" I bristled at his insult.

He shrugged. "I've eaten my fair share of cakes. You've done better."

I hated to agree with him, but I'd thought the exact same thing. Maybe it was the rosewater, or I simply hadn't whisked enough.

"Okay, that one's out," I said. "I wasn't sure about it, anyway."

"I was reading about a restaurant in London where the chef injects air into his food," Alice said. "Apparently, it's a new dieting trend. People go for this beautifully created food, and when they bite into it, there's barely anything there."

"That's a waste of a good meal," Campbell said.

I nodded. "And money. Why pay to eat air?"

"It's where the supermodels are dining." Alice glanced at Campbell. "Do you think I'm too curvy?"

His shoulders tensed. "I really couldn't say."

She grinned at me. "I eat too many of Holly's amazing desserts to be a supermodel. If I didn't like her so much, I'd think she was trying to fatten me up."

"I'd never do that."

She giggled. "My friend, Tabitha, wants us to go to this air food restaurant. She's always trying to drop ten pounds, even though she's already far too small."

"She should try cycling everywhere," I said. "It works wonders on the waistline."

Campbell adjusted his collar. It was one of the few times I'd seen him look uncomfortable.

I cut a slice off my caramel and vanilla sponge. "Campbell, try this."

"Me too." Alice grabbed the slice meant for Campbell and took a bite. "Oh my goodness. Heaven!"

Campbell chewed on the piece I gave him, his expression thoughtful. "This is good. It's caramel and something else. I can't put my finger on it."

"Good enough for the judging table?" I asked.

"You've almost got it with this one," he said. "And I agree about sticking to tradition. We don't want air-filled cakes presented to the Duchess."

"There's not a chance of that," I said. "I like real food full of amazing flavor. I was thinking about a Neapolitan and red velvet layer cake with a chocolate chip mousse. I'm having doubts. It might be too much."

"I like the sound of that," Campbell said.

"You'll have to come to the fair, Campbell," Alice said. "You can watch when Holly wins."

"Don't get ahead of yourself," I said. "There'll be a lot of competition. Just yesterday, I had three contestants come to the kitchen and try to find out what I was making."

Alice chuckled. "They're afraid of you. You're the one everyone's watching, Holly."

"Don't put pressure on me. I want this to be fun." But I did want to win. My baking was great, but it would be nice to get recognition. And I had the perfect place on the mantelpiece over my fire in my apartment where a little trophy would fit.

"So, Campbell, you'll be at the fair?" Alice asked.

"Of course, Princess. I'll be working there."

Alice sighed. "One day, I'll get you out with me when you're not on guard duty." She giggled, and a blush rose to her cheeks.

Campbell simply nodded.

"I was speaking to Lady Philippa the other day," I said. "She had some interesting thoughts about a problem that might occur at the food fair."

"Oh gosh, not one of her silly predictions," Alice said.

"Are they so silly?" I asked. "She was accurate when it came to the death of Lord Rupert's friend, Kendal."

"That's because she sees everything through those huge binoculars she's always peering through," Alice said. "Although she does sometimes see too much."

"Like the future?" I asked cautiously.

"Maybe. Don't go anywhere. I'll be right back." Alice dashed out of the kitchen before I could stop her.

I glanced at Campbell. He always made me feel like I was doing something wrong, even when I was on my best behavior. "Do you want to try more cake?"

"I'll have a piece of that Bakewell tart on the counter."

I handed it to him. "I'm not thinking of entering this, but it might be a nice addition to the café menu."

"It's good," he mumbled around the tart.

I placed my cutting knife down and busied myself with tidying away some equipment. I'd baked a dozen different options for the cake contest over the last forty-eight hours and wasn't happy with any of them. I shouldn't resist the Neapolitan and red velvet layer cake. It could be just what I was looking for.

Campbell finished his Bakewell tart and wiped his hands on a napkin. "You mentioned a problem Lady Philippa had predicted. What are we talking about?"

"I couldn't decipher it. She was cryptic." I tilted my head and paused in my tidying. "Do you have any thoughts on her ability to see the future?"

"Some. Nothing I'm prepared to share."

"Because you don't want to speak badly about a member of the family?"

"Lady Philippa has my utmost respect. It's not right to pass judgment on someone's ... eccentricities."

"What if she really can see the future? That would be handy in your line of work."

"Then she should be studied in a laboratory if that's the truth." He shook his head. "It's not possible."

"Here we are." Alice returned to the kitchen, clutching a large leather-bound book to her chest. "This is our family tree bible. I've been working on expanding it for months. It shows the deaths Granny foresaw."

My eyes widened, and I stepped closer as Alice flicked open the pages. "How many has she predicted?"

"At least twenty."

Eek! That was a worryingly high number.

"They weren't all old or sick when she made her predictions about their impending demise?" Campbell asked.

"Some were." Alice pointed to a family tree line. "My second cousin, Roseanna Belmore, dropped down dead one day. Granny predicted it would happen three weeks before the event. It turned out that Roseanna had a problem with her heart. She was into her riding and went out for a particularly hard hack and her heart couldn't stand it."

"And you're sure Lady Philippa knew this was going to happen before the event?" I asked.

"Absolutely! And take a look at this chap here." She pointed at the book again. "A great uncle of mine twice removed. He went traveling in India and contracted malaria. He died six weeks later. Granny predicted he'd get sick while traveling."

"That's not such a stretch. A lot of people get sick when they travel abroad." Campbell placed his hands behind his back.

"You're doubting my granny's word?" Alice arched an eyebrow.

"Lady Philippa's an incredible woman, but she cannot see the future," he said.

"She predicted this death, that death, that murder, and that person going missing." Alice jabbed a finger at different names on the family tree. "That's why we need to be so careful with her. We can't have her getting out and wandering around among the public telling them the dates of their deaths."

"Surely she's not that accurate," I said.

"She's accurate enough to convince me," Alice said. "What about you, Holly? Do you think my granny has special powers?"

"She's very convincing," I said.

"Whose death has she predicted this time?" Alice asked. "I hope it doesn't have anything to do with me or my family."

"She was vague," I said. "Pigs were involved."

Alice giggled and slapped a hand across her mouth. "Goodness, someone's going to be eaten alive by pigs. Whatever next? Maybe Granny's losing her touch."

"She also mentioned something about a hairpiece and figs. I can't piece it together. I wondered if it had something to do with the food fair."

"Let's hope not," Alice said. "I'm looking forward to wandering around and sampling the delicious treats. And of course, Campbell will be by my side guarding my every move, so I'll be in no danger."

Campbell nodded. "I won't stop you from enjoying yourself."

She waved a hand in the air. "I know that. You're marvelous at what you do."

"Whatever occurs at the food fair, neither of you need to be involved," Campbell said. "We don't want any more murders on our hands, do we, Miss Holmes?"

"Last time was an isolated incident." I tidied away the rest of my cooking equipment. "I'll stick to making cakes and keeping our visitors happy."

"And winning the competition," Alice said. "You've got to do that."

I smiled. "I'll do my absolute best."

Campbell grunted, not seeming satisfied with my response.

"Relax." I shoved more cake at him.

I didn't choose to poke around in trouble, but if it found me, I wouldn't back away and hide. Hiding wasn't in my nature. I was all about excellent cake, enjoying my life, and staying happy.

But from the glare Campbell gave me, I might not be happy for much longer.

Chapter 4

I stood outside my apartment and breathed in the crisp early morning air. Excitement rolled through me, as did a fair amount of nerves.

It was the morning of the food fair. The last three days had seen the arrival of marquees, sellers, and dozens of vans and food trucks unloading treats to sell to the public who'd be arriving in two hours.

I'd also be showcasing my cupcakes on the Audley Castle stand. I was looking forward to the visitors' reactions. I'd made a huge batch of chocolate and orange infused cupcakes with chocolate swirl icing.

"Woof woof?" Meatball nudged my leg before his nose lifted to the lush green lawn.

"Yes! Absolutely. We'll go for a walk before it gets too busy. I won't be able to have you in the marquee. But don't worry, I'll check on you regularly and make sure you don't go hungry."

"Woof woof!" He bounced on his paws before patiently waiting as I put his leash on, and we headed along the gravel path toward a main walking route around the castle. It was a good thirty-minute walk from my apartment to the

Coffee House Bridge and back, which would burn off some energy and stop Meatball getting restless.

I slowed to watch more sellers unload in the vendors' parking lot. I looked forward to spending my hard-earned money today and stuffing myself with delicious food.

"Mind your backs! The county's tastiest pies coming through."

I stepped to the side as a man carrying five white boxes strode past. He grinned and winked before heading to the main marquee.

I hadn't walked more than a dozen steps with Meatball, who was fascinated by the scents on the vehicles' tires, when the man returned.

He was tall, blond, with a sparkle in his bright blue eyes. He noticed me and smiled. "Will you be attending the food fair?"

I smiled back. "Yes. I work at the castle. I'll be on their stand during the day."

"A resident of the castle." His gaze ran over me and his grin widened. "Don't tell me I'm speaking to royalty? Should I bow and doff my hat?"

I chuckled. "There's no need. I only work in the kitchen."

"There's no only about working in a kitchen. I know how difficult it is to bake something that tastes amazing." He stuck out his hand. "I'm Pete 'the pie man' Saunders."

"Holly Holmes. Nice to meet you." I shook his hand.

"Likewise. I make the tastiest, most moreish meat pies around. You won't find anyone's pie that compares to mine." He tapped the side of his nose. "It's all about the secret ingredient. I never tell anyone the recipe. I'll take that to my grave. I get orders from across the world for my pies."

"They sound delicious," I said.

"They absolutely are. Hold on a tick." He disappeared into the back of a white van and emerged with a pie in his hand. "Don't take my word for it. This is pre-cooked. All you need to do is heat it in the oven." He went to hand me the pie, but it slipped from his fingers and landed pie top down on the ground.

"Oh! I'm so sorry." I stared forlornly at the pie. "That was my fault."

"Nope, that's on me. Butter fingers." Pete shrugged and smiled.

Meatball trotted over and sniffed the pie.

"But it looks like it won't go to waste," Pete said.

Meatball tried a mouthful of pie before his nose wrinkled. He backed away as if he'd tasted something he didn't like.

"That's odd. I guess he's not hungry," I said. "He's just had breakfast."

"He's probably not a fan of the spices," Pete said. "Sometimes, my pies come with a kick. I do a great chicken madras pie."

"That would be it. Meatball's not a fan of anything spicy," I said.

Meatball sneezed, his suspicious gaze lingering on the pie.

"What do you do in the kitchen?" Pete asked. "Head Chef?"

"No! I'm a general assistant, although I focus on the desserts for the café. I'm often out in the village, as well, delivering cakes to people."

"Someone as sweet as you must make delicious desserts. If you ever have any spare, I'm partial to something decadent. Eating dessert is such a naughty thing to do." His blue eyes sparkled. "Do you make naughty desserts, Holly?"

My cheeks felt warm. "I make an excellent death by chocolate."

"Maybe we could get together and you can tempt me with your treats." He waggled his eyebrows.

I continued to blush under his blatant flirting. He was a good-looking guy with a cheeky smile. "I expect you'll be too busy with your pie orders for anything like that."

"I always make room in my schedule for a beautiful woman."

"I'll be at the food fair. We can have a chat and a slice of cake later." It was time to friend-zone this lothario. He was a bit too smooth for my taste.

"We should make a time and a place for our sweet date," Pete said. "How about—"

"Pete, where do you want the lamb and mint sauce pies displayed?" A young woman with her dark curls pulled off her face in a ponytail hurried over. "There's barely any room left on the stall."

"We need to fit it all on. There are another dozen boxes in the van," Pete said.

The woman shook her head. "I knew we'd brought too many."

"Maisie, you worry too much. We'll have sold out by the end of the day," Pete said. He gave me another wink. "This is Maisie Bright, my catering assistant. Her middle name is panic."

Maisie's slightly harassed gaze met mine, and she nodded. "It's actually realistic. I'm worried the table won't take the weight of the food."

"Store some in the chiller cabinet in the back of the van. If it's slow going, I'll do a special offer. Four pies for the price of three. How does that sound? That'll get things moving."

Maisie sighed before nodding. "You're the boss."

"And don't you forget it." He rubbed his hands together. "Be a good girl and get more boxes out of the back."

Maisie bit her bottom lip but headed into the back of the van with no further comment.

Pete grinned at me. "She's a nice girl but doesn't have a clue about business. I'm helping her out by giving her this job. She's fresh out of college but eager to learn, that's the main thing."

"It's good you've taken a chance on her," I said. "It's more than a lot of businesses would do."

"Everyone needs a helping hand. Now, getting back to our hot date. How about—"

"This is where you've been hiding?"

Pete turned and the smile on his face faded. "Ricky! I didn't know you'd be here."

"More like you hoped I wouldn't find you hiding out here." Ricky wore scruffy dark jeans, a black leather jacket, and a white T-shirt. His attention turned to me and he smiled, exposing a gold tooth. "And who are you?"

"She's no one you need to worry about," Pete said. "What do you want, Ricky?"

"I need to have a serious word with you." Ricky inclined his head. "I don't expect you want your girlfriend to hear what I have to say."

I opened my mouth to clarify our relationship, but Pete shook his head discreetly at me.

"Let's go to the garden. It'll be quiet this time of the morning." Pete nodded a goodbye before hurrying away with Ricky.

That didn't look like it would be a friendly conversation.

I tilted my head as muttered curses and shuffling came from a food truck parked further along. I hurried over with Meatball. My eyes widened as a man teetered on the edge of the truck with a poorly balanced pile of boxes in his hands.

"Don't take another step." I dashed forward. "You're about to fall off the edge."

"Oh! Thank you. I can't see where I'm going." The man hidden behind the boxes sounded extremely posh.

"I'm going to take the boxes from the top, then you'll be able to see over and I can guide you down." I looped Meatball's leash over the handle of the truck door so he couldn't run off, then stood on my tip toes and grabbed three boxes. The delicious scent of basil and thyme drifted out of them.

"Is it safe to move?"

"Yes. Take a step forward and you'll feel the first metal step."

The man moved cautiously, peering over the top of the boxes. He let out an oomph as the boxes he held wobbled, but he made it down the steps safely. "Thank you so much. I'm on my own today and in a bit of a flap. My assistant called in sick. I was furious with him but determined to come to this fair. Then I was late. I got caught in traffic on my way. It seems like nothing's going right today."

"Well, now it is. I'll help you." I smiled at him. He was short and stout with a dark combover and bushy eyebrows. "I'm Holly. I work at the castle."

"It's the greatest of pleasures to meet you, Miss Holly," the man said. "I'm Dennis Lambeth."

"Nice to meet you, Dennis. And from the delicious smells coming from these boxes, you must be in the pie trade."

He smiled, his stern face lighting up. "Indeed I am. Hold on a moment." He set the boxes down and extracted a card from his pocket. "My great grandfather established Lambeth Fine Pies. He even delivered pies to the Queen."

"How wonderful to have such an established business."

He looked around and sighed. "The trouble is, people care nothing for tradition. They're only interested in how cheaply they can get their pies. My business has been struggling. It's all because these upstarts come along and undercut me." He gestured at the other food trucks.

"That's a shame," I said. "Some traditions should never die. Amazing pies definitely shouldn't."

"I couldn't agree more. I had to close a store in London six months ago. The rates had rocketed, and the overheads were crippling, but we were just hanging on. Then a hideous chain store opened up along from us. They do two-for-one deals in the evenings. I can't compete with that. I source ingredients from the finest suppliers and make sure the meat comes from farmers who care for their animals. These cheap suppliers import their meat from goodness knows where. They're most likely selling horsemeat pies and claiming it's the finest home grown beef." He shook his head. "Still, I shouldn't complain to you. These food fairs do me well."

Meatball was sniffing around the boxes of pies, his tail whipping back and forth.

I gently tugged him away. "Don't mind him, he has excellent taste when it comes to pies."

Dennis lifted the boxes off the ground, his gaze on Meatball. "I'm afraid he can't have any of mine. I need to sell all of these to turn a profit."

"Do you mind if I take a look?" I asked. "I work in the kitchens, and I've always got my eye out for inspiration."

"Be my guest." Dennis beamed with pride as I opened the box and gasped.

"They look beautiful." The pie lids glistened, and a tiny pastry bird sat on the top of each one. "These look so different from the other seller, Pete. He introduced himself as 'the pie man' and said his pies were the best around."

Dennis pushed the lid shut and scowled. "He's here! I'm surprised they'd have him. Has anyone tasted what he sells?"

I glanced over my shoulder at the pie Meatball had rejected. "Not that I know of. You don't approve of his pies?"

"I do not. He's a part of my problem. Customers have forgotten what real meat pies taste like. Mine are far superior."

Meatball whined and jumped at the boxes as if he agreed.

"You've definitely got one vote here," I said.

Dennis pursed his lips. "I just hope Pete's stall is nowhere near mine. We've come to blows several times. Pete's always telling me it's time to hang up my hat. I'll do nothing of the sort. I'm not prepared to give up yet. I'll beat him, no matter what it takes."

"Hopefully, you'll find plenty of customers today who know an amazing pie when they see one. I'll definitely grab my own."

Dennis huffed out a breath but nodded. "Thank you. That's appreciated."

I helped him carry the boxes into the main marquee, then took a moment to look around. There was a luxury Belgian chocolate stand, several cheese stands, ports and fine wines on display, a champagne stand, and a huge fresh fruit stall bursting with delicious ripeness. And that was just the first row of sellers.

My mouth watered. This would be an amazing event. I couldn't wait to be a part of it.

I was about to leave the marquee and collect Meatball, when I almost walked straight into a man wearing a baseball cap with a piece of cheese embroidered on the front.

"Excuse me. Let me guess, from that hat, you're selling cheese today?"

He bobbed his head and nodded. "Colin Cheeseman at your service. Before you ask, that is my real surname, and its appropriateness isn't lost on me."

Appropriate to his name, he had clumps of straw yellow hair sticking out from under his cap and pale blue eyes. He had a long face and a twitchy nose that reminded me of a giant rodent. He couldn't be more of a cliché if he tried.

I smiled warmly at him. "Do you specialize in a particular kind of cheese? I love a strong cheddar with pickle between two slices of freshly made bread."

A smile lit his face. "My cheese is something special. Come this way, you can take a look for yourself." He led me to a stall and stood beside it.

A variety of cheeses were laid out, but there was something different about them. For one thing, they didn't smell of normal cheese.

"Have you used a different kind of milk?" I asked.

"No milk at all. They're made from cashew nuts."

My eyes widened. "You make this out of nuts?"

"Why not? You can buy all kinds of nut milks these days. Why not a cheese alternative?"

"Is it an easy process to produce nut cheese?"

"Much easier than using cows' milk," he said. "People are moving away from dairy-based cheeses. They're high in bad cholesterol. With cashew nut cheese, you get an excellent source of healthy fats, protein, plus a delicious taste. Try some." He lifted a tasting board full of neatly cubed pieces of cheese.

I selected a piece and tentatively placed it in my mouth. A tangy rich flavor burst on my tongue.

"What do you think?" His nervous gaze was glued to my mouth as if he expected me to spit the cheese out.

I sucked the cheese slowly before chewing. "I could get used to this."

His hand shook as he lowered the tasting board, and he let out a relieved sigh. "It's the first time I've ever done one of these big events. And in such a grand venue. I was worried that people would think nut cheese was ridiculous and they wouldn't be interested."

"I'm interested," I said. "I'll have to buy some different varieties. You've got all sorts here." There were lumps of nut cheese studded with walnuts, dried cranberries, and dusted with black pepper. They looked delicious.

"I'm glad you like it."

"I love it. I'm selling cakes over on the Audley Castle stall. If anybody asks about cheese, I'll send them your way."

"That's good of you. Thanks. I almost didn't come. I felt sick with nerves this morning." His gaze went over my shoulder and he waved.

I turned and saw Pete strolling into the marquee with another two boxes of pies. He nodded at Colin.

"Do you know Pete?" I asked.

"We're good friends. He encouraged me to get a stand this year. He's tried my cheeses and is always pushing me to expand the business."

"From what I've tasted, you'll do really well today." Starting your own business was tough. I should know, having one failed café behind me.

He nodded. "Here's hoping. Good luck with your cake sales."

"And you. I'd better get going. I'll see you around." I left the marquee and hurried back to get Meatball.

We finished up our walk, and I returned to the kitchen, my thoughts on the soon to be open marquee that would be full of paying visitors.

After Meatball was settled with a bowl of water and a chew toy in his kennel, I had one final check of everything I needed for my own stall.

Laden with a huge trolley of goodies, I hurried back to the marquee. It was time to set up and let the food fair begin.

Today would be fun, and I'd be right in the middle of it.

I twisted my head from side to side and carefully rolled each foot in turn. There was less than an hour left of the food fair, and I was exhausted. I was used to being on my feet for a lot of the day, but add in the constant interaction with visitors eager to know about the castle and buy cake, and I hadn't had a moment to myself.

I'd managed a couple of short breaks, but other than that, I'd been on my own most of the day.

A smile crossed my face as I looked at the almost empty trays of cakes left from the busy day. Business was booming. Most people who came to the stand bought at least one cake, and everyone was delighted with the offerings available.

I lifted my head as a murmur ran through the crowd. People parted to let someone through. Lord Rupert appeared.

He ran a hand through his hair and grinned when he saw me. "Holly! How's everything going? Are you keeping the crowds happy?"

I glanced around at the people staring at Rupert. It wasn't every day they got to see a member of the Audley family strolling around.

"Everything's been great," I said. "Do you want to come into the stall? You're causing quite a stir."

He glanced around and shrugged self-consciously before dashing behind the table and hiding behind a large pull up banner. "Thanks. I sometimes forget that people think I'm something special."

"Well, you are a little special. You live in an enormous castle that you'll one day own."

He chuckled. "There's no guarantee of that. I had to come to the food fair. When I saw the crowds thinning out, I thought I'd risk it. Goodness, have you sold all these cakes?" His gaze ran over the empty trays stacked under the table.

"I have. I'm hoping Chef Heston will be happy."

"Lord Rupert, may I have your autograph?" A pretty blonde in a vest top and shorts thrust a piece of paper and a pen at him.

He cringed for a second before forcing a smile and nodding. "Of course. But you do know that I'm not famous."

"I think you're dreamy." The woman giggled and blushed. "And I can't believe you're not married. Are you looking for someone special?" She fluttered her long lashes.

He glanced at me as a blush crept up his cheeks. "I'm not ready for that. I'm still ... finding my feet."

"I'm sure you'll find them faster if you have someone special by your side," she said. "Do you prefer blondes or brunettes?"

"Oh, well, I think it's more to do with personality than hair color." He thrust the signed piece of paper back at her.

"Of course. Handsome and smart. You're the perfect combination." She giggled as her friends pulled her away.

A flicker of annoyance ran through me. Although I was also curious about Rupert's preference when it came to girlfriends. He'd been out on a few dates since I'd started working at the castle, but he never seemed enthused by the women he went out with. Maybe he simply wasn't looking for a relationship.

"Sorry about that." He grimaced and shook his head. "I don't know what people want with my autograph. They only do that sort of thing for rock stars, don't they?"

"To some, you are a rock star, especially to the women who want to marry a handsome prince and live in a castle."

"Gosh. Do you think I'm handsome?"

It was my turn to blush. I busied myself with straightening the leaflets on the stand. "I couldn't say. After all, you are sort of my boss."

"Oh, I'm not even close. I have nothing to do with the finances of the household. Chef Heston's your direct boss. I'm just a ... cog in the wheel."

I grinned. "I am the downstairs to your upstairs, though."

"No! Those days are long past. It's not as if we keep the staff hidden so as not to offend people. You're welcome in the castle any time you like. You don't even have to ask."

That was good of him to say, but I definitely would ask before I blundered into the family's private quarters.

"Here, try a piece of this chocolate and cherry tart before it's all gone. It's proved a hit with the customers."

"I don't mind if I do." He took the slice of tart and bit into it before nodding his approval. "Excellent as always."

His appearance was gathering a large crowd, and the last forty-five minutes were hectic as people came along pretending to be interested in picking up leaflets and buying cakes, all in the hope of getting a glimpse of Lord Rupert as he skulked at the back of the stall.

I looked around and gave a contented sigh as the last of the visitors trickled out of the marquee. It had been a great day. Busy and a bit stressful, but everyone had loved the food. I'd had nothing but compliments all day. It gave my baking ego a boost.

"Do you want a hand packing up?" Rupert popped out from behind a display.

"There's not much left to take back," I said. "As you can see, it's only crumbs on the trays. We've officially sold out."

"Then I'll pack those up and take them back to the kitchen," he said.

"You don't have to."

"It'll be my pleasure. After all, you're always delighting me with the desserts you make. It's the least I can do." He started packing up the trays, and I smiled as he worked. He was a decent guy.

I collected the few remaining leaflets and information on the castle and packed them in a box.

Rupert stood with the trays in his hands, staring at me.

"Is everything okay?" I asked.

"Yes. Perfect. I was just wondering, do you like opera?"

My eyebrows shot up. "I've never been. If I'm being truthful, I'm not a fan."

He shook his head. "Opera's not just about the music, it's the stories they tell. It's very dramatic."

My mouth twisted to the side. I was a rock 'n' roll girl through and through. I loved nothing more than the screech of a guitar and a throaty male voice. I couldn't see myself sitting at the opera listening to a warbling lady sing about death, heartache, and betrayal.

"Ah! I see I haven't tempted you with that offering," he said.

I blinked rapidly. Was that his attempt at asking me out? "Um, we could always compare music. We don't need to see an opera to enjoy it. You can stream some live and we can listen to it together. You might make an opera convert of me yet."

"Oh! I hadn't thought of that. We could do that. What kind of music do you like?"

"I'm a rock fan. Heavy guitars, loud drums, super confident lead singer."

"I've not had much experience of that kind of music. It all seems a bit … shouty."

"There are some amazing rock bands who've performed with symphony orchestras. I've got an incredible live recording of Lynyrd Skynyrd when they played with the San Francisco Symphony Orchestra. It'll blow your mind."

"Golly! That sounds intense."

"You can borrow it," I said. "Why don't you lend me some opera, and I'll lend you some rock? Our tastes can meet in the middle."

"That sounds fun. Then maybe we can—"

"He's dead!" a man yelled.

My head whipped around to see who was shouting.

"What did he say?" Rupert lowered the trays to the table.

"Somebody help me." Colin Cheeseman stumbled into view, his eyes wide and his body shaking.

I raced over and grabbed his arm. "Colin, what's the matter?"

He choked out a sob before raising a hand and pointing to Pete's stall. "Over there. I just found him." He leaned over and placed his hands on his knees, breathing deeply.

"You stay with him," I said to Rupert. I hurried to Pete's stall, my heart pounding. As I rounded the table and headed to the back of the stand, I froze.

Pete was on the ground with a pie slicer sticking out of his back.

Chapter 5

For a few seconds, I couldn't hear, see, or feel anything. Then everything snapped back into focus. Sound roared into my ears. I stumbled to the ground and checked for a pulse in Pete's neck.

There was nothing. He was dead.

Other stallholders followed close behind me, and the roar of chaos and people talking over each other began.

"Call an ambulance," someone yelled.

"Get the police."

"Is he dead?"

"What's that sticking out of his back?"

I shook my head and stood on shaky knees as I backed away. I looked around the stall, but there was nobody else there. Whoever had done this was long gone.

I turned from the horrible discovery and took in a deep breath. I looked at the gathered crowd of shocked people. Somebody needed to take charge of this mess. This was a crime scene.

I pointed to a man who had a phone in his hand. "Call an ambulance and get the police here."

He stared at me for a second before nodding and dialing on his phone.

"Everyone else stay back." I ushered the people away.

"What happened to him?" asked the stallholder I recognized from the chutneys and pickles stand.

"I'm not sure," I said.

"That can't be an accident," a woman said. "He didn't fall on his pie slicer, did he?"

"Most likely not," I said. "If this is a crime scene, we need to stay back and let the police do their job."

People backed away, muttering frantically to each other.

"Move aside. Security coming through." Campbell Milligan appeared through the crowd, followed by Saracen and two other security guards. His eyes narrowed when he saw me. "Saracen, get these people out of the way. Make sure no one tramples on potential evidence."

Saracen nodded and got to work with his colleagues.

Campbell turned to me. "What are you doing here?"

"I heard Colin yelling that someone was dead and came to investigate. That's when I found Pete." I gestured behind me, not ready to look at the body again.

Campbell looked over my shoulder, and his eyes tightened. "Do you know this man?"

"Not really. I met him today when he was unloading his pies. His name's Pete Saunders."

"Have you checked if he's still breathing?" Campbell was already moving, kneeling over the body, and his fingers going exactly where mine had been a few minutes ago.

"Of course. Someone's called an ambulance. The police will be on their way too." A wave of dizziness hit me, and I swayed.

Campbell was next to me in an instant, a large hand on my shoulder, stopping me from falling. "You need to get out of here."

I sucked in a deep breath as black dots sparked in my eyes. "He seemed like a nice guy. Why would anyone do this?"

"That's for us to investigate," Campbell said. "Leave here, now. Your interference isn't welcome."

My eyes narrowed as I glared up at him. "I'm not interfering. I'm helping."

"Help by staying out of the way. This is a murder scene."

I swallowed, feeling queasy. I forced my gaze back to the scene of the crime. Pete lay face down, his arms splayed out and his head twisted to the side. Several of his pies were scattered around him, as if they'd been thrown with some force. They were smashed all over the ground. Why would anyone do that to his pies?

Campbell gave me a less than gentle shove. "Time to go, Holly."

I took a few steps away, not sure what to do next.

Rupert appeared in front of me. He put an arm around my shoulders. "Let's get you out of here."

"Lord Rupert! You need to go with Saracen immediately," Campbell said.

"Oh, no, I'm fine," Rupert said. "I need to keep an eye on Holly. She must be in shock after discovering this terrible scene."

"Your safety is of paramount importance," Campbell said. "It's likely that this man has been murdered. The killer could still be on the scene. You're vulnerable."

Rupert's eyes widened, and he looked around the marquee. "I don't feel vulnerable. I want to take care of Holly."

"I'll be fine," I said. "Campbell's right. You shouldn't be here, just in case."

"Not without you," Rupert said. "Come with me to the castle."

I stepped out of his comforting embrace. "No, I'll be fine here."

"I … oh, well, if you're sure." He frowned, looking a little dejected.

"Really, you're much more important. You need to get somewhere safe."

Rupert scrubbed his chin as he was reluctantly led away by Saracen.

I stepped to one side and was almost knocked off my feet by a woman who barged through the watching crowd. She had a mass of silky dark curls. Her cheeks were pale and eyes wide as she stared around.

"Somebody said that Pete's been hurt. What happened? Tell me what's going on." She addressed her questions to no one in particular.

I caught hold of her arm. "Are you a friend of Pete Saunders?"

Her gaze flashed to me before she looked away. "Where is he? I need to know he's okay."

I bit my lip. I hated telling anyone bad news. "I'm really sorry to say he's not. He's—"

"Holly! Are you still here?" Campbell appeared beside me.

I huffed out a breath. "I was about to leave."

Campbell inclined his head toward the exit. "Good idea." He focused on the woman next to me. "Do you know the victim?"

I repressed a groan. Nicely done, Campbell.

She stared at him, and her mouth opened and closed several times but no words came out. She cleared her throat. "Victim? Pete's a victim? Please, I need to see him."

"No one can see him," Campbell said. "Not until we've collected any evidence."

The woman spluttered out several words but then nodded. "I'm not going anywhere. I have to know what's going on. You'll tell me eventually if I refuse to leave."

Campbell glanced at me and scowled.

I repressed a smile. It seemed he didn't like strong-minded women going against his wishes.

Campbell had just turned away when the woman leaped forward. She dodged around him and raced into the back of the stall.

She gasped before a wail shot from her lips. Then she was falling to the ground. Campbell caught her before she landed and lifted her without any effort before removing her from the scene.

As he dealt with the collapsed woman, I saw Colin. He was at the back of the crowd, looking pale and tense.

I hurried over. "Did you see who did that to Pete?"

He scrubbed at his forehead with his fingers. "No. I'd finished packing up my stall. I'd almost sold out so had little to do. I came over to offer Pete a hand, see if he needed any help with loading up the truck. I wandered in and ... found him on the ground." He sucked in a breath, and his jaw wobbled.

I patted his arm. "That must have been terrible."

"I didn't believe it. I thought maybe he was having a joke with me. Pete liked a good joke. Then I saw the blood and the mess. I tried shaking him but got nothing. Is he really dead?"

"I'm sorry, he is. You didn't see anything strange when you arrived at the stall? Nobody leaving or hurrying away?"

"Nothing like that," Colin said. "It was quiet. The crowd was thinning out. There was no one else around."

"Do you know the woman who just fainted?" I asked. "She knows Pete."

"Oh, yes, I know her. That's Jessica Donovan. They used to date. Well, an on-off relationship, I guess you could call it. Pete was popular with the ladies. I'd often be his wing man when we went out. She wanted to get serious, so he finished things. I'm not surprised to see her here today. She loves the food fairs. That's how they met, I believe."

"Did she still care for Pete?"

He nodded. "She'd often hang around when he was working and try to sweet talk him, but he wasn't interested. I'm sorry she had to see this, though. She's a nice lady."

I glanced around the watching crowd. Dennis Lambeth stood nearby, looking surprisingly smug.

He'd made it clear that he hated Pete and considered him a business competitor. A competitor that was putting him out of business. Had Dennis done something about that? He'd gotten rid of the competition by killing Pete?

I nudged Colin. "Do you know anything about Dennis Lambeth? I met him earlier today. He didn't seem happy with Pete being here."

"He wouldn't. They were always bickering. Dennis thought Pete ran a dodgy business. But Pete simply had lower overheads, so he could charge less for his food. Dennis marks up his pies because he claims they're such good quality."

"How deep did Dennis's animosity run? You don't think he'd do anything to Pete, do you?"

Colin blinked rapidly. "Dennis did this?"

I lifted a hand. "I'm just guessing, but it's not a bad motive."

He rubbed the back of his neck. "I don't know. Dennis was out of touch with the real world. I heard he had to close a store recently because he couldn't make a profit. I didn't realize things had gotten so bad. You think he lost his mind and stabbed Pete with his own pie slicer?"

"That's for the police to find out," I said.

"It's a tragedy," Colin said. "I was working with Pete on making a new pie. We were using his pie recipe and my nut cheese to make something unique. We made a great team." He wiped his eyes. "He was my best friend. All that's gone now."

I patted his arm again. "Did Pete have any enemies? Anyone who's threatened him or made him worried for his safety?"

"Other than Dennis?"

"Yes. Although I'm sure the police will talk to Dennis about their feud," I said. "Is there anyone else you can think of?"

Colin looked around the crowd, and his expression turned quizzical. "Where's Maisie?"

"Pete's assistant?"

He nodded. "I haven't seen her for a while. She's always so grumpy. Never happy unless she's complaining about Pete."

"She didn't like him?"

"Pete worked Maisie hard, and she hated that." He leaned closer. "Between you and me, I think she had a crush on Pete. Not that he'd do anything about it. She's almost young enough to be his daughter."

I hadn't noticed any chemistry between them in the brief time I'd met Maisie this morning, but Pete had been a charming, attractive guy. It was possible she had a crush.

Colin shook his head. "She was a typical young person and expected to have everything handed to her. Pete was having none of that. He made her earn every penny. She didn't appreciate it. I've heard her threaten to quit on numerous occasions."

My brow wrinkled as I pondered the possibility of Maisie being the killer. She'd have easy access to the stall, she'd definitely have access to the murder weapon sticking out of Pete's back, and he wouldn't have been suspicious about her being around.

I glanced at the crime scene. Was it really that simple? Had I figured out who the killer was thanks to my conversation with Colin?

If that was the case, should I tell Campbell and move on? After all, I had a cake competition to focus on.

It felt too premature to fix on Maisie as the killer. I'd do some investigating of my own before I passed on what I knew, just to be certain.

So long as Campbell didn't find out what I was doing, there wouldn't be a problem.

Chapter 6

I placed the last of the cake tins back in the cupboard and wiped down the kitchen surfaces in readiness for tomorrow's busy day.

I yawned and blinked my sleepy eyes. Today had been long and stressful. All I had planned for the evening was a long soak in the tub, followed by an evening curled up on the couch with Meatball snoozing by my feet. That sounded like heaven.

The kitchen door slammed open. Alice rushed in and grabbed hold of my hands. "Tell me everything!"

I resisted the urge to smile. "What do you mean?"

"No teasing me now." She tugged me over to the table and forced me to sit before joining me. "Rupert said you discovered the body at the food fair. How awful. I want to hear every detail."

I let out a sigh and nodded. Getting quizzed by Alice sometimes felt like one of Campbell's interrogations. "It was the last thing I expected to find among all those pies."

"And he was stabbed in the back with a pie slicer." Alice shook her head. "That can't have been hygienic."

"I doubt the killer was worried about getting pie crumbs in the wound. Maybe it was the only suitable weapon at hand. Although … there was something odd about the scene."

"What? Go on, tell me." Alice's blue eyes sparkled.

"The man who died, Pete Saunders, he specialized in selling pies. He even called himself 'the pie man' when we met. When I got to the murder scene, several of his pies were smashed. I thought maybe he'd been holding them and dropped them when he'd been attacked, but those pies hit the ground with force. They were obliterated. There were pieces scattered all over the crime scene."

"Maybe it was a disgruntled customer who returned the goods." Alice gasped. "I've got it! I know what happened to Pete. Someone tried to return the food they bought, and he refused to give them their money back. They threw the pies at him and things got ugly. The customer grabbed the pie slicer and stabbed Pete."

My nose wrinkled. "Would he have turned his back on an angry customer? Surely, he wouldn't have wanted to cause a scene in case it put off other customers."

"It's a good theory."

"It's an excellent theory, but I don't think that's what happened."

"How can you be certain?"

"I can't, but if you're right, we have a big problem. Hundreds of people visited Pete's food stall. Any one of them could have done it."

"Oh! That does complicate things. At least it happened right at the end of the day," Alice said. "It didn't spoil the food fair for everybody."

"It's always nice to meet a considerate killer," I said. "They made sure everyone got their meat pies and chocolate fudge before ending someone's life."

"There was chocolate fudge? Rupert never said anything about fudge."

I laughed. "One good thing about it happening at the end of the day was that not many people got to see. I expect it'll make the papers though."

"Of course. It's all over social media; I've been checking. This needs to be sorted out quickly. We don't want to put tourists off of visiting the castle. What's the next step in finding the killer?"

"Campbell's looking into it," I said. "Before I was shoved out of the marquee, the police showed up and they got together."

"You need to investigate as well," Alice said. "You're great at puzzling out mysteries."

"Campbell was very clear. He said no snooping."

"Don't worry about him. He's a pussycat. I'll get you in on his team. You just say the word."

"No! I'm not saying any word. Campbell will eat me alive if he catches me interfering."

"You're not a tiny bit interested in what happened to Pete?" Her grin suggested she knew just how intrigued I was about this murder.

I tilted my head from side to side. "There are a few possible suspects I've identified. And from the way Pete was killed, this feels personal."

"You think whoever killed Pete knew him?"

I tapped my fingers on top of the table. "That's exactly what I'm thinking. He had rivals at the food fair. Other sellers who didn't appreciate that he was undercutting their prices and taking their business."

"So, who are the suspects?"

I chewed on my bottom lip. "I met a friend of Pete's, Colin Cheeseman. He was selling his nut cheese at the fair today. He found the body."

"You think his friend killed him?"

"No, he seemed shocked by what happened. He was packing up at the time of the murder. Although it wouldn't do any harm to double-check where he was. But there was another man selling pies. A guy called Dennis Lambeth. He didn't hide his dislike of Pete and looked almost happy that he was dead."

"The rival pie seller murdered Pete." Alice nodded. "That makes sense."

"I have no idea where he was when Pete was murdered. I need to check that out. And then there's Maisie Bright, the unhappy assistant."

"An assistant! It would be easy for her to kill Pete," Alice said. "He'd have trusted her. He wouldn't have thought twice about leaving a deadly pie slicer in her hand. He turned his back, and then ..." She mimed stabbing in the air.

"And she's missing," I said. "I don't know if anyone's found her."

"She fled! She killed Pete and ran off."

I rubbed my chin. "It's possible. Anyway, like I said, I'm not getting involved."

Alice giggled. "It's too late for that. You've already identified several suspects. You don't want this murder going unsolved."

"It won't. Campbell's investigating." A scream had me jumping to my feet. "Where did that come from?"

Alice grabbed my hand and tugged me to the door. "Let's find out."

We dashed along the corridor and into Lady Audley's sitting room. Campbell stood in front of a champagne pink chaise lounge, his hands held out as he backed away from Jessica.

He glanced over his shoulder when we arrived, and his forehead wrinkled. "There's nothing to see here."

"He tried to kill me," Jessica squeaked, her dark curls a tangle around her pale face. "I woke up, and he was hovering over me. I thought I was a goner."

"That's not what happened," Campbell said swiftly. "You fainted again."

Jessica's eyes narrowed, and she glared at him. "You could be anyone. I wake up after having the shock of my life and find some huge scary man in a suit leering at me. What am I supposed to think?"

"He looks a lot scarier than he is." Alice hurried over. "Pay no attention to Campbell. He's my bodyguard."

Campbell cleared his throat as he took a step back.

Alice grinned at me and winked before turning her attention to Jessica. "Hello. I'm Princess Alice Audley. I live in the castle. This is my friend, Holly Holmes. She was at the food fair today."

Jessica glanced at me and recognition entered her gaze. "Oh! Yes, I know you. You were there when they found Pete. You were the one who told me ... you told me ... oh dear, I still can't believe it. This isn't some horrible nightmare I'm waking up from, is it?"

"No, I'm sorry to say it isn't," I said. "How are you feeling?"

"Sick to my stomach," she said. "When I saw Pete lying on the ground, I forgot to breathe. Everything went black. That's all I remember."

"Let me take over from here," Campbell said. "I need to speak to Jessica."

Alice waved him away. "No, she's clearly in shock. This needs a woman's touch. Holly, you take over the questioning."

I looked at Campbell. His eyes narrowed, and his fingers flexed as if daring me to get involved. "It might not be a bad idea if I ask a few questions. Under your guidance, of course. This must be a stressful time for Jessica."

Campbell gave a curt nod. "Go ahead."

I turned back to Jessica. "Do you mind answering a few questions about Pete?"

Her sigh came out shaky before she nodded. "Of course. If you think I can help."

"Were you dating?" I asked.

"We had been, but not for a few months," Jessica said.

"And Pete ended the relationship?" I asked.

"Oh, no. It was the other way round. I left him."

"Why did you leave him?"

"Because he wouldn't know the truth if it bit him on the backside. Pete was always hiding things. I tried to accept it, but he was always so secretive. Then I found a secret phone. That was the last straw."

"A secret phone?" Campbell stepped forward. "How did you find that?"

Jessica's cheeks flushed pink, but she lifted her chin. "When you don't trust someone, it makes you suspicious of their actions. I wondered if he was seeing somebody else. I began checking through his pockets to find receipts or evidence that he was cheating. One evening, I looked through his coat pockets and discovered another phone. That's the only reason I could come up with. He was hiding it because he didn't want me to see the messages from his other woman."

"Maybe it was a work phone," I said. "Pete's business was doing well. He wouldn't want to be bothered by work calls on his personal phone at all hours."

"That's not it," Jessica said. "He took calls about his business on his main phone all the time. Pete was rarely off that wretched thing. If he wasn't talking to someone, he was sending messages or checking in with suppliers. He never stopped working. Alongside all his secretive behavior and long working hours, I was pushed to the sideline. I had enough. I told him it was over and left."

"What did Pete think of that?" I asked.

"He made a few comments about trying harder and finding a better work-life balance, but I could tell he didn't mean it."

"It meant something to you?" I asked.

Campbell's foot nudged mine. "Perhaps asking about the murder might be helpful."

"I'm getting to that." I was trying to gain Jessica's trust and get her to open up. Plus, her relationship history with Pete was relevant.

She tipped her head back and her gaze traveled around the room. "Wow! I've only just realized where I am. This really is Audley Castle."

"It is," Alice said proudly. "It's my home. You're in Lady Audley's Sitting Room. It used to be a room only ladies could enter, but we don't follow that rule anymore. As you can see, Campbell's definitely not a lady."

"It's stunning," Jessica said. "Oh! I'm so sorry, I forgot my manners. You told me you're a princess. Should I have curtsied? Will I get in trouble for not following protocol?"

Alice giggled. "No curtsying required for any lady recovering from a fainting episode. You're fine as you are."

"Getting back to Pete," I said. "Did you want to get serious with him?"

Jessica shrugged. "When he was paying me attention, he was great to be with. He was funny and so charming. He could cheer anyone up."

"But only on his terms," I said.

"That's right. Everything was always on Pete's terms. I'd had enough. I'm not getting any younger. I want to find someone to fall madly in love with and have a huge family. It was hard walking away from Pete, but I needed to move on."

"And you moved on by visiting a food fair Pete was attending?" Campbell asked.

Jessica's expression hardened. "I was going to food fairs long before I met Pete. I'm not stopping something I love to do on the off chance I'll bump into him."

"There's a list of stallholders on the castle's website," Campbell said. "It would have been easy to check if Pete was here. Why come specifically to this one?"

"I didn't specifically come to this one," Jessica said. "I have a great aunt who lives in Audley St. Mary. She told me about the food fair. It gave me the perfect opportunity to come down, spend a weekend here, and go to the food fair. I didn't come because I was stalking Pete, if that's what you think."

I glanced at Campbell. I'd had the same thought about Jessica being an obsessed former girlfriend. It was a good motive for killing Pete. Jessica had been betrayed and let down. Pete's business came first, so she left him but couldn't let go. Had she been the one to kill him?

"Where were you at the time of Pete's murder?" I asked.

"I've been at the food fair most of the day. I always wait until the end because sellers mark down their produce so they don't have to take it all home. I was hanging around, hoping to get a good deal on some cakes when I heard people shouting. I raced over when someone said it was Pete who'd been hurt."

It wasn't the best alibi I'd ever heard, but it might be possible to check with other stall holders to see where she was.

"Where are you staying?" Campbell asked.

"My great aunt lives in Heatherfield Cottage," Jessica said. "Do you know it?"

"I do," I said. "I've gone past it dozens of times making deliveries. How long are you staying?"

"I was planning on leaving first thing tomorrow morning," Jessica said.

"It's best if you stay for longer," Campbell said. "I might have further questions."

He might? I'd been the one asking the useful questions.

Jessica frowned. "I can't hang around here forever. I need to be back to work in a couple of days."

"I can't insist you stay," Campbell said. "But if I have you arrested, you won't have much option."

"Arrested! For what? I had nothing to do with this." Jessica's bottom lip trembled.

I shook my head at Campbell's bluntness. This wasn't helping keep Jessica calm and cooperative. "Nobody is arresting you. But it would be easier if you stay for a few days. I'm sure your great aunt won't mind the company."

"Check my bags," Jessica said. "They're full of goodies. I got most of them within the last hour of the food fair. I wasn't waiting to get a glimpse of Pete like some love-struck teenager. I'm thirty-five years old. My days of crushing on unobtainable men are gone. I really was here for the food."

I looked over to see half a dozen bulging bags propped by the chaise lounge.

"Even so, stick around," I said. "You might remember seeing something that will be helpful in this investigation."

She nodded. "I can extend my stay by two days, but that's it. Then I need to leave."

"That might not be long enough," Campbell said.

"We'll have to make it do," I said to him. Jessica's arm trembled as it touched mine. She was still in shock. If we weren't careful, she'd faint again.

"May I go now?" Jessica asked. "Great Aunt Mary will be worried where I am. She might have heard what happened at the food fair and be panicking."

"Of course," I said. "How are you getting back?"

"I walked here," Jessica said. "The fresh air will do me good. I need something to clear my head after what's happened."

"Let me show you out." Alice took hold of Jessica's arm as she stood and collected her bags. "You can show me the things you bought at the food fair. I hope none of its spoiled."

Jessica's eyes widened for a second before she nodded. "Thanks. I never thought I'd be escorted anywhere by a princess."

As they walked away, the hairs on the back of my neck prickled. I turned to see Campbell staring at me. "I didn't do anything wrong. I was simply helping someone in distress."

"You were being nosy."

"Princess Alice forced me to come with her when we heard Jessica scream."

"Is that so?"

"Yes! And my questioning was useful. I got good information out of her."

Campbell crossed his arms over his chest and glared at me.

His intimidating stares wouldn't work this time. "I'm helping."

"That's enough of you being a Little Miss Cluedo. I've already told you to keep your nose out of this."

"I'm trying really hard to stay away. You're not making it easy, especially when you go around terrifying suspects."

"Is that so? So, you weren't in the kitchen with Princess Alice discussing suspects in this murder?"

I shook my head. Campbell's ability to overhear private conversations was worrying. "Only under instruction of Princess Alice, who insisted she know everything that happened. You're telling me to go against a direct command of our Princess?"

He smirked. "I've got a handle on this. We have our suspects and inquiries are being made. Evidence has been collected from the body—"

"Do you know exactly when Pete was killed?" I asked. "That could be helpful in ruling people out."

His nostrils flared, but he nodded. "At the most, he'd been dead ten minutes before he was found by Colin Cheeseman. People must have seen the killer go into that stall. We'll find them."

"I've no doubt you will," I said. "Maybe I can be useful. I've already thought—"

"Stop thinking." He pointed at the door. "Get back to the kitchen, and get on with your job."

My hands clenched into fists. I wanted to figure out this mystery, but I couldn't get distracted. Campbell was on the case, and I had a lot to do if I was taking part in tomorrow's cake competition.

"I can see I'm getting through to you," Campbell said. "Let's keep it that way. You focus on the cakes and—"

"I know, you'll focus on the security. I'm guessing you're heading up this murder investigation?"

"Naturally. We're linked in with the police and are working together. I'll have this solved within forty-eight hours."

"Good for you. I wish you all the best in your investigation." I didn't try to hide my annoyance as I turned and stomped away. I wanted to be a part of this, but I needed my focus totally on my cakes.

I had my reputation riding on this event. I couldn't let anything distract me. Muffins always came before murder.

Chapter 7

"Just three tiny hours." I followed Chef Heston around the kitchen. "That's all I need to get my cake finished in time."

"You should have done it yesterday," he said. "On your own time."

"I would have done, if it weren't for the fact someone was murdered." I'd spent two hours poring over recipe books last night and making my final decision over what cake to enter into the contest today. I was in two minds but had settled on the risky Neapolitan and red velvet layer cake. The problem was, I'd been so exhausted yesterday that I hadn't baked it.

Despite getting up two hours early and trying to get ahead of myself, I still didn't have enough time. And that had led me to begging Chef Heston.

He stopped so abruptly that I ran into his back.

He turned, placed his hands on my shoulders, and pushed me back. "You can have the time if you make me a promise."

"What's the promise?"

"That you win."

I sucked in a deep breath. There was no way I could promise that. The competition would be tough, and I had no idea what the other cakes would be like. Most likely gorgeous. They'd blow mine off the table.

"I'll give it my best shot."

"No, you'll win. You work for Audley Castle. You work in my kitchen. It's not just your reputation on the line. If you lose, my judgment will come under scrutiny."

"I promise, I won't even mention you. I won't say anything about the kitchen. I can enter under a false name if that's any help. You don't have to be associated with my baking."

He tutted and shook his head. "You're an excellent baker."

"Thanks. That's nice of you to say. Now—"

"But if you don't win, you'll be pulling double shifts with no extra pay. And I'll make sure you get all the peeling duties."

I grimaced and looked away. I hated peeling vegetables. However, I needed this time. It was either accept the deal or pull out of the contest. And I was no quitter.

"Okay, I'll win this competition."

He glanced at the clock. "Your three hours start now."

"And I'll take my lunch break when the judging takes place," I said.

He flapped a hand at me. "Don't make me regret this."

I grinned as I raced away and gathered the equipment I needed. I was setting up and measuring out my flour and sugar when Betsy Malone hurried into the kitchen.

Her eyes lit up, and she dashed over. "Everyone's poking around and asking questions about the murder at the food fair."

I kept my gaze on the recipe in front of me as I placed ingredients into a large mixing bowl. "I bet they are."

She leaned closer, the faint smell of lemon cleaning polish drifting off her clothes. "When I was coming into work today, a shady guy stopped me. He wanted to know what I was doing going into the castle and did I work here?"

I paused from my frantic measuring and looked at her. "A shady guy? Was it a reporter looking for a scoop?"

"No. At least, he didn't look like one. He didn't have one of those plastic tag thingies around his neck with his press credentials on."

"What did he look like?"

"Dark, sinister. He wore a leather jacket. I smelled trouble." Betsy sniffed.

That sounded like Ricky, the man who'd spoken to Pete the morning before he died. "What was he asking you about?"

"When he found out that I cleaned at the castle, he started interrogating me about who they thought killed Pete. As if I'm supposed to know anything like that. I'm not one to gossip."

I smiled affectionately at her. Betsy was one of the biggest gossips I knew. She got all the best gossip because of her ability to glide silently through the castle, cleaning without getting in the way. When people thought they couldn't be overheard, that's when the juicy secrets came out.

"What did you tell him?" I cracked eggs with one hand as I continued to skim through the recipe.

"I told him it was none of his business. I said he should stop asking questions or someone might think he had something to do with it."

I grinned. "What did he say to that?"

"He scuttled off, especially when I said I was on first name terms with the head of security. He didn't like that one bit."

"Was he asking about suspects because he hoped the police had charged someone? If he's involved, he won't want the police paying him attention. They won't do that if they have a suspect in their sights."

"I can't answer that. But he had a bad look about him," Betsy said. "I didn't trust him an inch. And, I was down the pub last night, just having a soft drink, mind you. I'm not one for alcohol."

I suppressed a smile. I had to keep my cooking sherry away from Betsy when she was in the wrong mood. I'd heard all about her antics at last year's employee Christmas party. She definitely liked to drink.

"Did you hear something useful?" I asked.

"I should say." She leaned closer. "There was this horribly smug little man standing at the bar. He was telling the story of how he saw Pete's body. Everything he was saying was so gruesome. It turned my stomach."

"He must have been in the crowd after Pete was discovered."

"Either that or he did it. He was talking in great detail about a silver pie slicer sticking out of the man's back." She shuddered and pulled a face. "It was disgraceful. And the worst thing was, he kept saying that he deserved it. He told everyone within earshot that Pete wasn't a nice man and cheated everyone he knew. He had it coming."

"Do you remember what this man looked like?" I asked.

"Short, a little dumpy, dark hair with a combover. Small dark eyes. Another one not to be trusted."

That sounded like Dennis Lambeth. He needed to be more discreet about saying Pete deserved to die or the police would take a long hard look at him if they weren't already.

"Anyway, I can't stop. Still a dozen rooms to clean. You be careful, young Holly. There's a killer on the loose." She patted my arm.

I nodded. "Don't worry, I'm not involved in this one. I'm entering the cake competition today."

"Best you do something fun and safe like that," Betsy said. "It's a nasty business." She nodded before bustling out of the kitchen.

I mulled over what Betsy had told me as I continued to mix the ingredients for my cake. It was very possible that Ricky or Dennis were involved in this murder.

Dennis hated Pete, and his business was in trouble. And when Ricky had spoken to Pete, his tone wasn't friendly. Could they have been involved in a business deal gone bad? Had Ricky been here to collect on a debt and Pete refused to come good? Whatever it was, Ricky and Dennis needed to be on the list of suspects.

I slowed my vigorous mixing. Should I tell Campbell about this? He'd warned me to keep out of the investigation and would only accuse me of snooping if I told him this information. But it might lead him right to the killer.

I focused on my batter, beating it to ensure the sponge would be light and fluffy. I was just getting the familiar burn in my biceps telling me that I was almost done with my whisking, when the kitchen door was pushed open.

Campbell marched through, his shoulders tight around his ears and his hands clenched. "Come with me."

This sounded like trouble. I shook my head. "No can do. I'm at a crucial stage with my sponge whisking. If I stop now, I'll lose the air."

"Then lose the air. You're needed." He turned and walked away.

I was tempted to ignore him, but his tone was deadly serious. I hurried after him, continuing to whisk my cake batter, keeping the bowl wedged under my arm. I pushed the door open with one hip and walked into the corridor to find Campbell waiting.

He turned, glanced at the cake bowl, and shook his head. "There's been a security situation. I'm needed elsewhere."

"What happened?" I don't know why I asked. Campbell would never tell me.

"A member of the family has been ... compromised."

"Compromised how?" It sounded like I was in the middle of a spy movie.

"That's on a need-to-know basis. I have to leave immediately. You're to fill in as my temporary assistant."

My eyebrows shot up. "Temporary assistant of what?"

"I need you to speak to the remaining witnesses in the Pete Saunders murder."

I nearly dropped my mixing bowl. "Is this a joke?"

"We've already established that I don't make jokes."

"I'm not trained. I don't know how to question people. What if I mess up?"

"You might not be trained, but you notice things, and people seem to like you. We've made inroads in this investigation, but I need to take most of my team from the castle to deal with this other matter. That leaves a skeleton crew to ensure the family's safety. They can't deal with this investigation as well. Here's a list of people you need to talk to." He thrust a piece of paper at me.

I had no free hand to take it. "Tuck it in my apron pocket. I'll have a look when I get a moment."

"You need to make more than a moment for this," he said. "I might not be back for a few days."

"This sounds serious," I said. "It doesn't have anything to do with Lord Rupert, does it?"

"That's on a—"

"I get it. It's need-to-know, and I definitely don't need to know. Or do I?"

"Correct. It's not your business. All you need to do is ask the questions on that sheet of paper. Establish where people were, what they thought of Pete, and if they had any motive for killing him. That's it. You can't mess that up, unless you do anything foolish."

"I never do anything foolish," I said. "Are you certain you want me to do this? Maybe you should get someone from the local police to speak to the remaining suspects."

"This matter is under my jurisdiction," he said. "The police do what they can, but there's only three of them covering the village. I've informed them that you're my assistant. They'll be there as backup should you need them, but it's a simple operation. You won't need to arrest someone."

"I will if I get a confession."

"You won't. It's never that simple. Gather the information and pass it to me. And before you get ahead of yourself, this is temporary. I'm leaving Saracen in charge of overall castle security. That means he's also in charge of you."

I gulped. Saracen in charge of me. He barely talked and was super scary, almost as terrifying as Campbell.

"Can't Saracen ask the remaining suspects the questions?"

"Saracen has a specific ... skill set. It's not dealing with people."

"Is it killing dangerous types with his bare hands and hiding the evidence?"

"It's worse. He's your liaison. Update him twice a day. If you find anyone who causes you alarm, tell him. He'll deal with it."

"Will the person still be alive after he's dealt with them?"

Campbell tilted his head slightly. "It's fifty-fifty odds they will come out unharmed, but it's the best I can do in this situation. Are you with me on this?"

It was less than ideal. I had my cake competition to focus upon. But I was interested in getting to the bottom of this mystery. Still, I wavered.

"Holly, are you in?" The urgency in Campbell's voice snapped me to attention.

"I'm in. But make Saracen promise he won't scare the life out of me."

"I can't promise that. Saracen has a particular way about him. It works. He gets the job done. Don't mess around and stay out of his face, and you'll get through this in one piece."

Eek. That was a terrible guarantee. "But what about—"

Campbell held up a finger. "Go ahead, Alpha two."

I couldn't hear anything. Sometimes, I could hear the other end of Campbell's conversation when he spoke into his sleeve mic. They must be in silent mode so they wouldn't let slip what this mysterious security situation was all about.

I burned with longing to know. It sounded intense and exciting. Maybe I'd taken the wrong career path by becoming a baker. I could have been a super spy, just like Campbell. But if I did that, I'd miss the baking. I doubted you got the guarantee of triple chocolate brownies every day when you were on a spy mission to save the world.

"Understood. Out." Campbell lowered his sleeve. "Walk with me." He turned and strode along the corridor.

I had to jog to keep up with him, being careful not to let cake batter slop over the sides of the mixing bowl. "I'll do what I can, but I've got the cake contest this afternoon. I'm not abandoning that."

"I'm not asking you to. Fit the questions in around work, but make sure you complete your mission. Don't let me down." He pulled open the door and strode toward the helipad behind the castle.

"I won't." My heart raced and a smile spread across my face. I was a former secret agent's assistant. Did that make me an assistant secret agent? Agent in training? Probably more like Campbell's lackey.

"I'm trusting you, Holly." Campbell turned and walked away before I had a chance to speak. He slid into a sleek black helicopter, and it took off.

It was so James Bond, I couldn't help but be impressed. Maybe Campbell thought I could be valuable to him after all.

I turned and hurried back to the kitchen. I'd solve this mystery and prove that I was a valuable asset.

I pulled open the door and yelped as I staggered back, the cake batter slopping all over my arm.

Saracen stood in the doorway, blocking my entrance. His eyes were masked by sunglasses, and his bulky frame strained the seams of his black suit. His dark hair was cropped short and his shoulders were so wide they almost touched the doorframe.

"Um, hi there. I believe you're looking after me while Campbell's gone," I stuttered.

Saracen nodded.

"That's great. I'm busy right now with my Neapolitan cake, but we can get to solving Pete's murder later. Does that suit your schedule?"

He nodded again.

Was I going to get any words out of him?

"Well, okay. That's brilliant. Come on Saracen. To the kitchen. We have a cake to bake."

Chapter 8

"Hold it delicately between your index finger and your thumb, like you're holding a thin piece of glass." I tried to keep annoyance out of my tone. Saracen was close to breaking his sixth iced miniature rose, and it was my last spare. "Keep it steady, then I'll surround it in icing and stick it to the cake."

Saracen grunted, and a bead of sweat trickled down the side of his face.

I'd been surprised when he'd followed me back to the kitchen this morning, but he'd been my silent and efficient baking assistant for almost three hours.

I'd expected him to snap as I'd kept bossing him about, but he liked taking orders. It must have been due to his military training. As long as I was clear and succinct and didn't give him options, he did exactly what I told him.

I had decided to expand Saracen's knowledge into the fine art of cake decorating. The problem was, he was anything but delicate, and trying to get him to hold a tiny pastel pink rosebud without shattering it was proving tricky.

"That's it. Hold it right there. Don't move. Don't even breathe." I swiftly iced the flower into place and stood back as my gaze ran over the cake.

Six layers of sponge perfection sat in front of me. Two layers each of chocolate, strawberry, and vanilla sponge. They were stacked on top of each other and filled with generous alternate layers of vanilla cream and chocolate chip mousse. The outside was coated in more cream and the top dotted with a bouquet of tiny blush pink rosebuds.

"Okay, that's got it. We're ready to take the cake to the viewing table before the tasting session begins."

Saracen stood against the wall and clasped his hands behind his back.

"Do you want to come and see the other cakes with me?" I asked.

He grunted.

I'd quickly learned that sound meant he wanted me to tell him what to do, not give him an option. "You're coming with me. We're taking the cake and having a look at all the other contestants' entries. Let's go."

Saracen instantly moved and opened the door for me as I carefully held the tray containing my cake.

We walked toward the marquee where the contest was being held. I found the table with my name on it and slid my cake carefully to the center.

I brushed my hands together as I turned and surveyed the marquee.

There were twenty cake entries on display, alongside the savory treats, beverages, and sauces and chutneys.

My confidence wavered as I studied some of my competition. There was a tower of angel cakes on a table of glitter and tiny white angels, several traditional fluffy sponge cakes, a big meringue dish covered in fresh berries, and a chocolate roulade.

My mouth watered and my stomach grumbled. I'd been so busy concentrating on my cake that I'd forgotten to eat lunch. At least there'd be plenty of leftovers to enjoy after the tasting had finished.

My gaze shifted as I spotted Maisie hurrying along the other side of the marquee. She was on Campbell's suspect list. "Saracen, you guard the cake. Don't move."

He adjusted his position and stood in front of the cake, his head swiveling from side to side as if checking there were no enemies creeping up and about to attack.

I hurried over to Maisie, surprised to see her standing by a stall with her name on. Beside her was a large pie topped with a pastry lid.

"Hey, Maisie. I didn't know you were entering the contest."

She shrugged and glanced at the pie. "Why not? Since I'm here and that security guy doesn't want me going anywhere, it seemed like a waste not to make the most of it."

"You're entering one of Pete's pies?"

She snorted a laugh and shook her head. "Of course not. Those pies were nothing special, just generic meat pies with an unidentified filling. I rarely ate the freebies Pete gave me. Way too salty."

"You didn't enjoy the pies you sold?"

"Did you try one of Pete's pies?" she asked.

"No, although he gave me one to try. I dropped it on the ground. My dog wasn't keen on eating it, though. Meatball normally loves anything like that."

"Then your dog has excellent taste," Maisie said. "Pete's pies were bland. He used spices and salt to give them flavor. I decided to enter my very own recipe. This is my pie. My recipe. My entry."

"That's great," I said. "How are you feeling after what happened to Pete?"

"Not great. It was horrible."

"Have you been questioned about what you saw?"

"I spoke to that scary security guy yesterday. He took my details and said he'd be in touch."

"I'm helping him with the investigation," I said. "Have you got time to talk now?"

"Oh! Sure. I didn't know you were a part of the castle's security team." Her gaze went to my cake stand.

"This is a ... freelance assignment," I said.

She shrugged. "What do you need to know?"

I tried to remember the questions Campbell had put on the piece of paper he gave me. "What did you think of Pete?"

Maisie looked at her pie. "Pete was a charming cad. When he wanted something, he'd turn on the charm. Once you'd been around him a while, it was easy to see it was just a front. That wasn't the real Pete. He played a character. Once he'd gotten what he needed, he dumped you."

"Which you didn't approve of?"

"It annoyed me that people never saw through it, but I was the same. He promised me all sorts when I joined his business. Did I get to see them? Not a chance."

"What was he like as a boss?"

She frowned. "Boss! More like I was his slave. The job wasn't great. He took advantage of me and my eagerness to get work experience and a decent reference. He used me just like he used everybody else. Do you know how he paid me?"

"Minimum wage I'm guessing."

"That would have been nice. Pete paid me in leftover food. He gave me those horrible pies and said they'd see me through. I forced down a few, but only when things got desperate. He was a bad boss. I was thinking of leaving but wanted to get another month or two of experience before I cut loose from the situation."

"You weren't romantically involved with Pete?" I asked.

She tipped back her head and laughed. "That's a horrible thought. There was no way I'd have dated Pete. He was a good-looking guy and had that roguish charm he used. It worked on most women, but he was a fraud. Besides, he was old enough to be my dad. I might like a mature guy, but there's mature and then there's disturbingly old."

So much for my thoughts on an unrequited love gone bad. "Do you know of anybody who had a problem with Pete? Anyone who might be angry enough to kill him?"

"I don't know. I mean, he rubbed a few people up the wrong way, but only when they found out he'd used them. Most of the time, people were oblivious to what he did. Sure, he put noses out of joint, especially with the special deals he'd roll out when we'd get a job lot of cheap pies. Most of the other sellers simply couldn't keep up."

"Any recent arguments that stand out?"

"No, nothing new. He'd always talk them around, buy them a pint, and that would be an end to it. I can't think of anyone who'd be angry enough to sneak into the food fair and stick a pie slicer in his back."

"May I ask where you were yesterday? I noticed you weren't around when Pete's body was discovered."

"I'd worked alongside Pete most of the day," she said. "He ordered me to start loading up the van because the crowd was thinning out. I was walking backward and forward between the marquee and the truck. That's when he was killed. Loads of people would have seen me."

"I didn't see you," I said. "And I discovered Pete's body. You didn't appear the whole time I was there."

She looked away. "Oh, well, I didn't like to say, given that I'd been handling food all day, but I had an upset stomach. I blame one of Pete's nasty pies. Anyway, I had to make an emergency dash to the loo. I was probably gone twenty minutes. When I felt better, I came back to the marquee. That was when I saw what had happened. I didn't see you. You must have gone by then."

That wasn't a great alibi. I'd be able to check if Maisie was seen loading up the truck, but there was no way I could know for certain if she'd been in the toilet that whole time.

"When you got back to the stall, did you see anything strange or out of place?" I asked.

"Aside from Pete's body and the mess?"

"Yes. Had any money gone missing or anything like that?"

"You're thinking a robbery gone wrong?" Maisie shook her head. "No, we wear these satchels around our waists and keep the money in it to stop anyone with light fingers. I have one, so does Pete. His was around his waist. None of the money was taken according to the investigator."

"So, nothing missing?"

She twisted the end of a curl around one finger. "His laptop wasn't there. Pete always had it open and posted on his social media pages about how amazing his pies were. When I got back, it had gone."

I couldn't recall seeing a laptop on the counter when I'd discovered Pete, but I'd been so shocked, I could have missed it. Would someone kill a person to get their hands on a laptop?

A murmur from the other contestants in the marquee had me turning, and I gulped. The Duke and Duchess were by my stand, examining my cake!

I took a step toward them, then froze to the spot. I'd gotten distracted by Pete's murder and forgotten all about my entry.

"Thanks, Maisie. Good luck with your pie." I dashed over, trying to calm my racing heartbeat as I neared.

I slowed and tilted my head. Saracen was talking to the Duke and Duchess. I'd never seen him so animated. He was smiling, nodding, and waving his arms around. Whatever had possessed him?

As I drew nearer, I could hear what he was saying. He was describing my cake like a professional chef.

"The sponge is especially light because of the special whipping technique. It's whipped first by hand and then machine. It's that extra effort that adds the lightness."

"This is possibly the lightest sponge cake I've ever tried," the Duchess said.

"The decorations are made by hand. Each rosebud was expertly crafted by the skilled designer. She glued each one on individually," Saracen said.

"And where did you say the filling was from?" The Duke examined the cake, bringing a piece to eye level and squinting at it.

"The fruit's locally sourced. You get a perfect mix of tart and sweet from the strawberries," Saracen said.

"It's absolutely delicious," the Duchess said.

Saracen caught my eye and winked. "And you'll be pleased to know the baker of this wonderful cake has just arrived." He gestured me over before standing to one side.

I still couldn't believe what I'd heard. I stuffed down my shock and smiled brightly at the Duchess and the Duke. "I'm sorry I wasn't here when you arrived to look at my cake."

"That's quite all right," the Duchess said. "Your ... assistant was very helpful. Although he looks awfully familiar. He must have an identical twin who works in the castle security team."

Saracen ducked his head.

The Duchess smiled indulgently. "Not to worry. We all need hobbies to indulge in. It's good to learn my security have other interests. It's important to have a well-rounded character."

"He's been a great assistant," I said.

"You've done wonders with this cake, Holly," the Duchess said. "Light, just the right level of sweetness, and entirely moreish. This will be hard to beat."

"I'm glad to hear that," I said. "I wanted to make something classic but memorable."

"You've definitely done that." The Duchess touched her husband's arm. "Let's move on to the next stand, my dear."

"Just one more piece of this cake before we go," the Duke said.

"Save your appetite," the Duchess said. "You need to keep a clean palate so we give everyone a fair chance."

The Duke reluctantly placed his piece of cake down. He nodded at me. "The best yet." He wandered away with his wife.

I turned to Saracen, still tingling with shock and surprise. "You do speak in complete sentences."

He shrugged. "Only in emergencies."

"This was definitely an emergency. I got distracted. I saw Maisie and got talking about what happened to Pete."

"What did she tell you?"

"That she was unwell at the time of the murder, and Pete's laptop is missing."

Saracen nodded. "Interesting."

"Would someone have killed him for his laptop?"

"That depends what's on it."

"What do you think could be on it?"

"Blackmail files. Dodgy pictures. Records of corrupt business dealings. Threatening letters. Anything's possible."

A talking Saracen was much more fun. I cut off a large slice of cake and handed it to him. "My way of saying thank you for promoting my cake."

He grinned and scooped the cake up before biting into it.

I blew out a breath and looked around the marquee. My cake had been tasted by the first round of judges. There were two more judges coming to sample my entry, then it was up to all of them to vote on their favorites.

From the comments the Duke and Duchess had made, I was hopeful I'd get placed. Even if I just got a rosette, or a highly commended, that would be enough. Although I remembered Chef Heston's threat. If I didn't win, it was double shifts and peeling duty.

"Are you happy to stay with the cake?" I asked Saracen. "There are two more judges coming to taste it, and there's someone I want to speak to."

He nodded, his mouth full of cake.

I hurried back to the savory section and over to Colin Cheeseman's table. "Hey, Colin. I didn't know you were entering."

"I need to get the word out about my cashew nut cheeses," he said. "I didn't want to miss out on this. Getting a commendation from the Duchess will do my reputation wonders."

"And how are you holding up?"

He sighed and adjusted the cap on his head. "I'm still in shock. I mean, it's only been a day and so much has happened. Is there any update on what's going on?"

"I'm sort of helping with the investigation, actually," I said. "I wondered if you could help me confirm a couple of alibis."

He nodded. "Of course. Anything that can help. Who's in the frame for this?"

"There are several people we're interested in," I said. "Did you see Maisie around just before Pete was murdered?"

He glanced over to her table before looking away. "I saw her at Pete's truck not long before I found him. We weren't parked far from each other. She was loading something in the back. Although it was busy at that time, and I was focused on getting my own things packed away."

"Could you have missed her going back to Pete's stand if it was so busy?"

"It's possible. I wasn't looking out for her in particular. Despite her faults, she's not a bad girl. She just has a bit of growing up to do, but she'll get there. I can't see her as the killer."

I couldn't either. Maisie seemed like a bright, intelligent young woman. Although she'd been clear that she wasn't happy that Pete had paid her in leftover meat pies. Despite that, she seemed calm and level-headed. Maisie was going places.

I mentally shifted her to the bottom of my suspect list.

"What about Pete's ex-girlfriend, Jessica?" I asked. "Did you see her around Pete's stall?"

Colin shook his head, and his bottom lip wobbled. "I didn't see her. I mean, I saw her earlier in the day. She was browsing the other stalls, but I don't know if she made contact with Pete while she was at the food fair. Pete would have only been nice to her if they'd met. He never liked to make an enemy. If he ever had an argument with anyone, he was quick to smooth things over. He was just that kind of guy." The wobble in his voice suggested he was close to breaking down.

"How much longer are you staying?"

"I have a sleeping area in my food truck, so I can stay as long as needed. I'm going to see some potential clients with my nut cheese while I'm here to make the most of my visit."

"Your business sounds like it's doing well," I said. "That must be exciting. Focus on the positive. I know this is a horrible time, but you'll get through it."

He looked around, his face full of despair. "It feels different now. I'm not sure I'll keep doing these food fairs. It was Pete who pushed me into this event. He always was the confident one, up for a laugh and making me try new things. I was his calm anchor. Sometimes, Pete got a bit outrageous, but I ensured he didn't cross the line. I'm not sure I'll find anyone to have fun with again."

The poor guy. I felt so sorry for him. "Wait right there." I hurried back to my stand and cut off another piece of cake before returning to Colin and handing it to him. "This won't solve all your problems, but cake always makes me feel better when I'm sad."

Tears filled his eyes, and he blinked them away. "That's kind of you. Thank you. And if there's anything I can do to help with the investigation, please do ask. I keep going over it in my head to see if I missed anything, but nothing springs to mind. It's still a mystery as to what happened."

"It's a mystery I plan to figure out. Don't worry, we'll get this solved soon enough."

He bit into the cake and smiled at me. "Let's hope so."

I nodded goodbye and hurried back to my table. I needed to narrow down my suspects. It looked like Maisie was out, but Jessica was still in the frame if I couldn't confirm her alibi. Then there was the shady business partner, Ricky, who was still snooping around. That was suspicious. And Dennis Lambeth, who'd been vocal about his dislike of Pete. It had to be one of them.

I just needed to figure out a way to find the proof, so I knew who did it.

Chapter 9

"Wake up!"

A hand shook me from my slumber. I groaned and rolled over, coming face-to-face with Princess Alice. Her blonde hair was tied off her face in a high ponytail, and she wore what looked like pajama bottoms, a vest top, and a bright pink hoodie.

I blinked several times. "Is this a dream?"

She giggled. "No, silly! I've got you a surprise."

I yawned and checked the time. "Alice! It's six o'clock in the morning."

"Which is the perfect time."

I groaned. "For what?"

"Your special surprise. I almost couldn't get in your apartment to give it to you," she whispered.

"Why not?" I sat up and rubbed my eyes. "Did Meatball try to bite you for breaking in?"

"No! He licked my face." She glanced over her shoulder. "Did you know that Saracen's guarding your front door?"

"What? No! Why is he doing that?"

"Maybe he has a crush on you." She giggled behind her hand. "He is awfully tall, though. I imagine you don't even come up to his chest."

"I've never gotten that close to measure," I said. "He's not as scary as I first thought. He was a big help yesterday at the cake competition."

She grinned. "And the results will be out this morning. I hope you've made the finals."

I felt conflicted about that. Part of me did want to be in the finals, but that meant a lot more baking, which would take me away from figuring out Pete's murder.

I loved baking, but the thought of this unsolved murder hanging over my head loomed large. As much as I wanted to focus on my delicious desserts, Pete deserved justice.

"So, you mentioned a surprise," I said.

"You're going to love this. But we need to sneak out. We don't want Saracen getting in the way."

"In the way of what?" I petted Meatball as he hopped onto the bed and came over for his morning cuddle.

"I'm not telling you any more. Get up and dressed. Wear something stretchy." Alice backed away from my bed.

"What are you playing at?" I rolled out of bed and downed the glass of water I kept on my nightstand. I pulled out some comfortable yoga style workout clothes before heading into the attached bathroom.

"I'm playing at being amazing," she said as I closed the door and had a quick freshen up.

I emerged five minutes later after washing my face and brushing my teeth. "How are we going to sneak past Saracen if he's outside?"

She pointed at the stone wall. "Easy. The same way I got in. We use the priest passages."

My eyebrows shot up, and I grinned. "You have secret hiding places in the castle walls?"

"Of course. I spent my childhood racing around them with Rupert."

"How do we get into them?" I'd learned about priest holes and tunnels during my studies. They'd been created in the sixteenth century to hide Catholic priests during a time of persecution. It wasn't uncommon for many great estates to have them. Some were simply spaces behind walls, while others were larger rooms and passages, allowing the priests to slip away without being caught.

I stared at the solid brick wall she walked toward.

"We shuffle our fingers behind this brick and press down hard." Alice wiggled her eyebrows, and a slight grating sound drifted toward me. A lump of stone slid away from the wall, revealing an entrance.

I hurried toward it and stared into the gloom. "Where does it lead to?"

"They go off in all different directions. You're lucky to have one in your apartment. They don't all have them. This can take you to most of the castle if you know the way. But most importantly, it will take us outside."

I pulled on my sneakers, grabbed a white baseball cap to hide my bed-messy hair, and hurried after Alice.

Meatball whined as he poked his nose into the tunnel. I scooped him up to make sure he didn't get lost. Once he was tucked into my arms, he seemed as intrigued as I was.

Alice pulled out her phone and used the torch function to light the way as we hurried along the gently sloping stone passageway. It was narrow—you could only fit one person at a time—and the ceilings were low and smelled of damp.

"It's horrible to think of all those poor priests who were forced to hide in places like this," Alice said. "According to the old family record books, there were places where food and ale was left for the priests so they could survive in here for weeks."

I shivered. "That couldn't have been much fun."

"Better that than be killed. It wouldn't just be the priest who'd get in trouble if they were caught. The owners of the castle would be punished for harboring fugitives. There are records of beheadings, imprisonments, and hangings in my family. It was a terrible business. Still, the passageways are fun for us now. We get to sneak in and out and don't have to answer to Saracen. You need to have a word with him about what he's doing outside your apartment. You don't want people to gossip that you're having an illicit fling with a member of the security team."

Yikes! I hadn't thought about that. "I don't know why he's out there. I didn't ask him to wait for me."

"Maybe he's in love." Alice giggled.

"Less of that," I muttered.

"He's not your type?" She turned a corner, and I hurried to keep up with her.

"I prefer my men a little less ..." I wasn't sure how to describe my taste in men. Eclectic could work.

"Terrifying? Able to kill with a single blow?" Alice asked.

I chuckled. "I'm sure Saracen will make someone the perfect husband, but it won't be me."

"Here we go. This is the exit we need." Alice fumbled against the wall for a few seconds before another door opened, leading to the outside. She grabbed my hand. "This way. We don't want to be late."

I stumbled into the clean, fresh air of a summer's dawn. The castle looked so beautiful, standing majestically in the still peacefulness of the new morning.

A bleating sound drifted in the air, and I tilted my head. "What was that?"

"Woof woof?" Meatball squirmed in my arms.

"That's your surprise. Come on." Alice tugged me along.

We rounded the corner into the private family garden, and I skidded to a halt. In front of me was a long-limbed, tanned woman dressed in designer yoga gear.

She smiled and nodded as she saw Alice.

But my attention was taken by the four pygmy goats wandering around the garden.

"I don't get it," I said. "What are we supposed to do here?"

Alice lightly smacked my arm. "I know you love all things bizarre when it comes to fitness. We're having a session of goat yoga."

I stared at the goats and then at Alice. "That's a thing?"

"Of course it's a thing," she said. "There are all kinds of benefits to goat yoga. Our mats are waiting, as are the goats."

She led me over to a mat, and we both bowed to the yoga instructor.

"Namaste," the woman said. "I'm Natalie. I'll be your instructor this morning. Our four assistants are these delightful goats. Today, we have the privilege of working with Miss Daisy, Clover, Bubbles, and Murphy."

Meatball shifted in my arms, his intense gaze on the goats.

"Are they experienced in working with novices?" I watched the little goats scampering around.

"They are patient with all abilities," Natalie said. "Trust the goats. They're naturally inquisitive and will enjoy joining you during this session of yoga. Are you both ready to begin?"

I gulped. "I guess so."

"We absolutely are," Alice said.

I grinned at her enthusiasm. Yoga with goats could be fun. And Alice was right, I did have a weird interest in fitness trends. I was always looking for the one thing I could do that I enjoyed so much it didn't feel like exercise.

Natalie's gaze went to Meatball. "You may find it easier to do the poses without your companion."

"Oh! He should be okay with the goats." I placed Meatball on the ground.

He immediately bounded over to the goats, his tail up and his whiskers quivering.

A small black and white goat lowered her head and butted him in the side.

"Woof!" Meatball jumped back before trying to sniff the goat's backside.

He got another couple of head butts, but after some more sniffing they settled next to each other.

"We shall begin by lying on our backs, holding our knees against our chests and rocking slowly from side to side," Natalie instructed us in a calm soothing voice. "This stretches out your muscles."

I laid and rolled. It was relaxing to be outside in the fresh morning air, no noise other than the gentle bleating of goats.

"Stretch your legs and place them gently on the ground," Natalie said. "Put your arms either side of you with your palms up. I want you to take five deep breaths, in through your nose, filling your lungs, and then out through your mouth."

I'd just taken my second large inhalation, when a small goat bounced on my stomach and bumped the air out of me.

"Oomph!" A pair of curious eyes met mine. "Hello to you." I patted the goat.

The little chap bounced up and down several times before jumping off and scampering away.

"That was Murphy. The goats will interact with you when they sense you have a need for extra support," Natalie said. "They also stand on you when you need extra weight to be tested in a particular pose."

"Isn't this marvelous?"

I glanced over to see Alice cuddling Clover. "I thought this was goat yoga not goat cuddling. Is that allowed?"

"Of course it is." Alice nuzzled her nose against the goat's head.

Natalie nodded. "People gain comfort from the goats in different ways during this practice. The goat will tell you when you've had enough physical contact and you can move seamlessly into the next move. When you're ready, roll onto your hands and knees, and we'll move into the cat pose."

"More like the goat pose," Alice said as the goat bounced away from her.

I settled on my hands and knees and tried to align myself as I was bounced on by yet another goat.

While I was trying to even out my weight and settle into a secure pose as the goat wobbled on top of me, Meatball wriggled under my belly, rolled onto his back, and stared up with an adorable look on his face.

I lowered myself and kissed his belly several times. "You've got nothing to worry about. I'm not falling in love with the goats."

Meatball licked my chin as I rose back into the cat pose. He remained where he was, wriggling backward and forward to get my attention.

"When you're ready, slowly lift the opposite arm and leg and hold that pose for thirty seconds. Keep your core tight."

I was constantly wobbly as the goat bounced on my back and Meatball wriggled beneath me, trying to get more belly kisses. I'd never felt so challenged during yoga.

"Lower that arm and leg and repeat on the other side," Natalie said.

"Phew!" Alice collapsed as Bubbles bounced on top of her.

"This isn't as easy as I thought it would be," I panted, sweat developing around my hairline.

We ran through several more poses, Meatball and the goats competing for my attention as we did the downward facing dog, the salute to the sun, and the cobra.

"Time for a five-minute break," Alice said. "I'm exhausted from all this goat exercise."

"Who knew little goats could be so heavy." I flopped onto the mat and cuddled Meatball as he squirmed onto my stomach, still jealous of all the attention the goats had been paying me.

"Are you having fun?" Alice asked.

"Yes! This was a great idea. Thanks for thinking of me when you planned it."

She waved a hand in the air. "You needed a way to de-stress. Campbell has put a lot of pressure on your shoulders. I have to make sure my favorite baker doesn't crack. I'd miss my brownies too much if you went into therapy."

I had to chuckle. "Well, I'm grateful for my goat experience."

"So, any progress?" Alice crossed her legs and leaned toward me.

Clover ambled over and bounced into her lap.

"I'm still asking questions and trying to figure out who'd most want Pete dead."

"Are you leaning toward anyone in particular? Did Granny's message about figs and wigs not help?"

I scrubbed my fingers through Meatball's fur. "Not really. I'm not sure how it can be related to this murder. Pete didn't sell fruit."

"Did he sell fig pies?"

"He only did savory pies."

"Do figs and meat go together?"

"It's not a combination I've tried to make. And even if they do, where does the wig fit?"

Alice played with Clover, who hopped around in her lap. "Campbell must trust you to figure this out on your own."

"He doesn't expect me to solve this. I'm just his information gatherer."

"Wouldn't it feel great if we did solve it for him, though? Imagine his face when he gets back, and the murderer has been arrested, and it's all thanks to us."

My eyes narrowed. I wasn't all that keen on Alice getting involved in this mystery. With the killer still out there, it put her at risk. It also put me at risk, but I wasn't in line for the throne.

"Investigating murder isn't a job for a princess," a deep male voice rumbled.

My shoulders tightened, undoing the excellent work of the yoga instructor. I turned to see Saracen standing next to a bush, his hands clasped in front of him.

"Oh, Saracen! You silly thing." Alice climbed to her feet, Clover cuddled in her arms. "Of course, I wasn't suggesting I go hunting for a killer. I'd issue instructions from a safe distance. You don't need to worry about me."

"It's my job to worry," he said.

Alice giggled and looked at me. "Isn't it wonderful having all these dreamy men protecting me? I feel positively spoiled."

"It must be great." I stood, my gaze still on Saracen. Would he think this was my fault, and I'd snuck Alice out of the castle?

"You should join us," Alice said. "You look like you hold a lot of tension around your shoulders. Goat yoga is just the cure you need to get rid of that."

A series of expressions flashed across Saracen's face before the usual blank mask slid into place. "Goat yoga wouldn't be appropriate while on duty."

I bit my lip to stop from smiling and turned away. "I found it very relaxing."

Alice nodded enthusiastically. "Isn't it? We shall have to do it again. Maybe we could get our own goats at the castle. We could have private sessions whenever we liked. We could get everyone involved, Saracen included."

"I'd definitely come along to that." I glanced at Saracen. His shoulders definitely looked tight now.

Miss Daisy trotted over to him, took one look at the man mountain, and sprung in the air, obviously mistaking him for a summit she needed to reach.

Saracen's arms shot out, and he caught the goat mid-flight.

The goat gave a startled bleat before nestling into Saracen's arms and butting her head against his solid chest.

"See! You're a natural with the goats," Alice said. "You must be a part of our goat yoga team."

Saracen carefully set Miss Daisy back on the ground before returning to his stiff guard position.

"Goodness, what's going on here?" Rupert ambled around the bushes, still dressed in what looked like his pajamas. He had on an oversized white T-shirt and a pair of checked pants. His hair looked like he'd recently stuck his finger into a plug socket.

"Goat yoga," Alice said. "I arranged it for Holly."

"I didn't know you liked goats," he said to me.

"Sure. What's not to like? These are particularly cute."

"Well, that's an interesting thought." Rupert scrubbed his hands through his hair. "Goats, eh? I always knew you liked animals."

"You're right. I love all animals," I said.

"Good to know." He nodded at Saracen. "How's the investigation going into what happened to that chap at the food fair? Got any leads?"

That was something I needed to get back to.

"We're figuring it out," Alice said. "We'll have it sorted before Campbell comes back. He'll be so proud of *us*."

Saracen quietly cleared his throat and shook his head.

Alice waved a hand in the air. "You know what I mean. We'll be very safe and there is zero risk in solving this murder. Come on, Holly. We've got forty minutes of goat yoga to finish."

I shook my head and backed away, even though I was tempted to spend more time with the cute goats. "I should go. I've got a busy day."

"Oh! That's a shame. I distracted you by talking about that silly murder. Rupert, you take Holly's place," Alice said.

"Oh! Goat yoga. I'm not sure I'm coordinated enough." Rupert looked cautiously at Bubbles, who was repeatedly head-butting Saracen in the shin.

Alice grabbed Rupert and dragged him over to the mat. "Of course you are. Stand upright, hold your core muscles in, and remember to breathe deeply. There's nothing to it."

"It sounds complicated," he said.

"You'll be great," I said. "I'll leave you to it." I didn't glance at Saracen as I hurried away.

I half-expected him to grill me about how I'd snuck out of my apartment without him noticing, but he didn't say a word as he followed Meatball and me.

Maybe he knew about the secret passages or had a tracker on me, so he'd detected my movements as soon as I'd left. He'd been trained by Campbell, so that was a definite possibility.

I had to refocus. It was time to get sleuthing and baking.

Chapter 10

"Good news, Holmes." Chef Heston slapped his hand on the counter. "You made the finals of the food fair competition. Congratulations."

I stared up at him from the stack of cupcakes I was decorating with chocolate icing, not sure I'd heard him right. "How do you know?"

"Because I'm your boss. I know everything. You're one step nearer to avoiding double shifts. Good for you." He smacked me on the back before striding away.

I hurried to finish the cupcakes, a riot of nerves and excitement turning in my stomach. I'd done it. My entry was good enough. I was through to the finals. But that left me with a complication. Should I set the murder to one side and focus only on my baking to ensure I won?

All day at the back of my mind, the suspects in Pete's murder had churned away. Why had Pete been killed? Who had the opportunity? What was the reason he'd been murdered? Where was his laptop? Who was the last person to see him alive? So many questions. I felt like I was barely getting started. And now, I had a baking final to prepare for.

I grabbed the tray of chocolate cupcakes, stumbling as I turned too quickly.

A strong hand steadied me by the shoulder as another grabbed the tray and took it from me. It was Saracen. Where had he come from? The last time I'd seen him, he'd been walking out the kitchen door. When had he come back? He was like a silent, giant ninja.

I blew out a breath. "Thanks. My mind's not on the job."

"Thinking about murder?"

I glanced around the kitchen, but everyone else was too busy to listen in. "Pretty much. Good cake save."

"Where do you want these?" he asked.

My eyebrows rose. "They need to go out to the café. The serving staff will know what to do with them."

He disappeared with the cakes and returned a moment later. "All done. Ready to focus?"

The talkative version of Saracen was back. "Absolutely. I need to get baking my entry for the contest. I made it through to the final."

"I meant questioning more suspects about Pete's murder."

"Oh! Well, that's also important." I tugged at my bottom lip. "Please, can we do the baking first? You can help if you'd like. You were useful the other day."

"I squished most of your rosebuds."

"But we got through. It was a joint effort. And I find your presence surprisingly calming, considering how deadly you are."

"What makes you think I'm deadly?" The corner of his mouth slid up.

"You work for Campbell."

He raised a shoulder. "I can spare a little time for baking."

"Great! Just let me beg off a couple of hours from Chef Heston. You can be my backup if I need it."

"You want me to rough him up if he tries to make things hard on you?"

I stifled a laugh. That would be hilarious and was tempting. "Maybe don't beat up my boss. He'd definitely hold it against me." I raced off, and after much pleading from me and sighing from Chef Heston, I was given two hours to work on my design concepts for the contest.

I clapped my hands together, getting that familiar bubble of excitement as I embarked on a baking adventure. "I've got two recipes. The first one is a red velvet mousse piped into fresh eclair cases and topped with a cherry and chocolate ganache."

"Sounds good," Saracen said.

"My second option is a dark chocolate and rosehip torte with an apricot glaze and gooey chocolate center. That might be too cutting-edge for the contest though. I've already made the eclair cases and the tart base, so it's really focusing on the fillings and getting the combinations right."

"Will you need a taste tester?" Saracen asked.

I grinned at him. "Absolutely."

"Show me what you need to make this happen. I'm already hungry."

We spent ten minutes arranging the ingredients for both desserts. I was soon whipping up the red velvet mousse, which was a combination of clotted cream, sugar, fresh vanilla from vanilla pods, and crushed strawberries and raspberries to add color and depth.

I set the mousse in the fridge to set and turned my attention to the tart bases. I'd created six bases, knowing how tricky short crust pastry could be to get right. I selected the most perfect one and placed it in front of me.

"What now?" Saracen asked.

"How's your stirring arm?"

"My ... stirring arm?"

"You need a steady eye and a strong stir to get this right." I placed chocolate chunks in a glass bowl over a saucepan of simmering water. "Keep stirring until the chocolate is melted and lump free. Be careful not to let the bottom burn or the chocolate goes bitter."

"Stirring, no lumps, avoid the burn. Got it."

He was the perfect assistant.

I added the filling to the tart, topped it with a lattice of sweet pastry, and placed it in the oven. "That'll need twenty minutes. I'll whip up the toppings and filling for the eclairs, and then we can head off and talk to our next suspect."

"Who do you have in mind?" Saracen asked.

"Ricky," I said. "Have you had anything to do with him yet?"

"Hold on." Saracen pulled his phone out of his pocket and raised it to his ear. "Go ahead, boss."

I strained to hear the other end of the conversation but couldn't. I wouldn't be surprised to learn Campbell had been listening in on our conversation this whole time. Now we'd gotten around to talking about something he was interested in, he got in touch.

"Got it. We'll get to work on that." Saracen placed his phone back in his pocket.

"Anything of interest?" I asked.

"Campbell wanted an update."

"You didn't tell him anything."

"He already knows everything that's gone on."

I swirled a finger in the air. "Because of the listening devices he's placed all over the castle?"

Saracen pressed his lips together.

I nodded. "They're everywhere, aren't they?"

"Why would that be true?"

"Because Campbell likes to snoop."

"Wrong."

"He does!"

"He ensures the safety of some very important people."

"Which means he gets to listen to everything?"

Saracen shrugged.

I shook my head. "I know my rights."

"And they are …"

"No snooping! Especially not in my private apartment." I leaned closer. "He doesn't have any listening devices in there, does he?"

Saracen simply smiled and continued to stir the chocolate.

"That will do." I took over and tested the chocolate. It was perfect. "This needs cooling, cream, and whipping."

"How long will that take? Campbell suggested we hurry up. I agree."

"Give me fifteen minutes for the tart to cook, then we can go out while everything's cooling and find Ricky."

"Where are you planning on looking?"

"The pub. A reliable source spotted him there recently."

"You believe he's still in the village?"

I tilted my head. "I do, although he might be keeping a low profile if he was involved in Pete's murder."

"What makes you say that?"

"He was snooping around the castle asking questions. That suggests he has an interest. Maybe he wants to make sure someone's charged so that the finger of suspicion doesn't point at him."

Saracen grunted. "He sounds guilty. Let's start with him."

Once the tart was done, I left it on the side to cool, grabbed my jacket, and headed out with Saracen to the only pub in the village. I felt like royalty as he drove us in an enormous sleek black SUV used to transport the family.

The Parson's Nose was a large building with an enormous thatched roof and a huge open fire at one end of the pub. Dark beams dominated the ceiling and were decorated with dried beer hops.

Saracen stood in the pub doorway and looked around. "Where's our suspect?"

My eyes brightened as I saw Ricky. "This way." I headed toward a hunched figure at the bar, nursing a pint of ale.

"Ricky Stormy?" I asked him.

He didn't look up, but his shoulders tightened and his hand clenched around his glass. "Who wants to know?"

"We do," Saracen said.

Ricky's head shot up, and his gaze ran over Saracen's imposing form. "And you are?"

"He's here to ask you a few simple questions," I said. "I work with castle security, and we're investigating the death of Pete Saunders. I believe you knew him."

"Nope. You're wrong."

I pursed my lips and tried again. "I saw you talking with Pete the morning before he died."

"You're mistaking me for someone else." He took a large gulp from his pint glass before setting it back on the bar.

My brow wrinkled, and I studied him carefully. This was definitely the guy I'd seen talking to Pete. "I'm Holly Holmes. I sort of knew Pete. What can you tell me about him?"

"Not a thing. And I don't care who you are." He shoved his stool back and stood. "I was trying to have a quiet drink. It looks like I need to go elsewhere."

"We haven't finished with our questions."

"Not my problem." He rapped his knuckles on the bar. "You should be careful who you let into this pub," he said to the barmaid, Elspeth Samphire. "No one wants to come here to be interrogated." He strode to the door.

Hmmm. That hadn't gone as I'd hoped. Before I had a chance to plan my next move, Saracen strode along behind Ricky and followed him out the door.

I raced after them, my heart thudding. I didn't want things to get physical, but I really did need to speak to Ricky.

I stepped outside. Ricky was almost jogging in his haste to get away from Saracen.

Saracen continued to march after him, his long strides keeping pace with Ricky.

"Leave me alone, man," Ricky yelled. "I can't help you. I don't know this guy you're talking about."

I ran after them. "We're trying to discount you from the investigation. All you need to do is answer some questions."

"I know nothing. Get out of my face."

"Do you want me to take this goon down?" Saracen muttered as I caught up with him.

"I don't want you to cause him any harm," I said. "But he needs to stop running. It's making him look guilty."

"Agreed. Let's put an end to this." Saracen broke into a jog.

Ricky turned as Saracen closed the gap between them, and his eyes widened. He danced back on his feet as he raised his fists. "I know my way around the boxing ring. Don't make me knock you on your behind." He jabbed out a fist.

Saracen avoided it, dodged behind Ricky, and gripped him around the back of the neck with a large hand.

Ricky squirmed and squealed as he was marched back toward me.

I stared at them with wide eyes. Ricky's face was bright red and sweat trickled down the side of his face. Saracen looked like a picture of calm. Talk about thriving under pressure.

"Thanks for that, Saracen," I said.

"Let go of me, you loser," Ricky growled out. "You can't keep me against my will. Call off your guard dog."

"This won't take a minute," I said. "Since Pete was your friend, you'll want to help us find out what happened to him."

"We weren't friends." Ricky twisted his head and glared up at Saracen.

"If you promise not to run away, Saracen will let go," I said.

Saracen grunted.

"Fine. I won't go anywhere. Ask your dumb questions," Ricky said.

"Excellent. Thanks for being so helpful." I nodded at Saracen. He gave Ricky a squeeze and let him go.

Ricky scowled at him as he rubbed the back of his neck. "That'll bruise. I should sue you."

"You don't need to sue anyone," I said. "Tell me about your relationship with Pete."

"We didn't have a relationship," Ricky said.

"You knew him?"

"In a way. It was no big deal."

"How did you know each other? Were you doing business together?"

"What do you want to know for?" Ricky's nostrils flared.

"Because he was murdered at the castle's food fair. We have to find out who did it."

His grin was sharp. "And that bunch of stuck up toffs have you investigating the murder? Good luck with that."

"I have plenty of backup if I need it." I glanced at Saracen. "Don't make me set him on you again."

Ricky lifted his hands and sighed. "Whatever. I came here because I knew Pete would be attending. The idiot got his name on the list of stallholders. I had an alert set up on my phone whenever his name appeared online, so I knew he'd be here."

"And why did you want to see him?" I asked.

"He owed me money. I'd loaned Pete cash to open a pie store. I needed it back. Pete knew the terms of our agreement but was dragging his heels when it came to making his repayments. He kept coming up with lame excuses. I didn't care about that. I wanted my money. I figured meeting in person and having a friendly little chat about his obligations would see us right. Then the idiot gets himself killed. I still want my money."

"You won't get it back now," I said.

He shrugged. "I'll find a way. Pete had assets."

"You're going to steal Pete's belongings?"

"It's not stealing. He's repaying a debt he owes me."

"How much did he owe you?"

"Thirty thousand. He needed it to pay for stock, lease, and do a basic refit. It seemed like a good deal. The guy had a sound business. At first, everything was straightforward, but then he stopped taking my calls. That's never a good sign. Then the first payment was late, followed by the second. I don't let people get into debt with me for long."

This was an excellent motive for murder. Pete decided not to pay back the money he owed Ricky. Maybe he'd paid Pete a lesson and reminded him what would happen if he didn't repay, and things got out of hand.

"Where were you when Pete's body was found?" I asked. "I don't remember seeing you at the food fair."

"Nah! I hate those food fairs. All that overpriced rubbish that you can get in the discount stores for much less. It tastes just as good. I only came here to have a chat with Pete and get what I was owed."

"You weren't at the food fair when Pete was killed?" I asked.

"Nope. I was in the pub."

"All day?"

"I went in about three in the afternoon. I had business to take care of in a nearby town so went over there, got that sorted, and then returned. I took a look in at the food fair to make sure Pete was still around and then headed here. I chatted up a cute barmaid most of the afternoon. She has it bad for me."

"And you didn't leave the pub at any time?" I asked.

His eyes narrowed. "Oh, I get it. You're pointing the finger at me for Pete's murder."

"Well, he did owe you money. And he was being slow at paying it back."

"Yeah, all true, but I'm not an idiot. Killing someone makes it hard to get back what you're owed. I've been known to rough up a few people when they welch on a deal, but murder isn't me. I loan money, and I collect money with a healthy rate of interest on it. That's most of my business. Do I break a few kneecaps along the way? Now and again. Murder's not in my repertoire."

I shuddered at the thought of a broken kneecap. Ricky sounded like he had an appetite for violence. "If it wasn't you, who do you think would want to kill Pete?"

"I can tell you exactly who killed him. Pete had a serious rival. A posh bloke called Dennis. I even saw him at the food fair."

Dennis Lambeth was already on my suspect list. "Did you see them together at any time during the food fair?"

"You bet I did. I saw them arguing. And it got physical. Dennis is hardly Muhammad Ali when it comes to fighting, but he still shoved Pete around and called him all kinds of names that I'd never repeat in front of a lady." Ricky grinned at me. "That guy was jealous of Pete's success. He's losing money and trade and is furious about it. If anyone wanted Pete dead, it was Dennis. That's your killer. You're wasting time by trying to get a confession out of me."

"Do you know what they were arguing about?" I asked.

"I couldn't hear. I was too far away. I just saw it was them. But it was bound to be the usual thing. Pete always undercuts Dennis's prices. He gets his supplies from a different source."

"What source?"

Ricky tapped the side of his nose. "Dennis was always riding Pete's back about his inferior products and claimed his pies were nothing better than dog food."

I swallowed, glad I'd never gotten around to trying Pete's pies.

"How bad are things with Dennis's business?" I asked. "I learned he had to close one of his stores not so long ago."

"And there'll be more closures. You'll have to ask him yourself how bad things are, but I don't expect him to be in business in a year's time."

I blew out a breath and glanced at Saracen, who'd been standing stoically next to Ricky this whole time. We'd just found the next suspect we needed to speak to.

"So, am I free to go?" Ricky glanced at Saracen. "You're not gonna set this meathead on me?"

"Sure, you can go. Just don't leave the village," I said.

"I can't stay around for much longer. Two more days here and I'm out."

"Not before we discount you as a suspect," I said.

"Yeah?" Ricky took a step toward me. "You're gonna stop me, are you?"

"No, I'm not going to do anything," I said. "But I'll happily send Saracen out to find you."

Saracen took a step toward Ricky and glared at him.

He scarpered backward. "Fine, fine. I've still got some business locally. But if you want to find out who did this, talk to our angry, almost bankrupt pie maker. He wouldn't have thought twice about burying the pie slicer in Pete's back and laughing while he did it." Ricky shot one more glare at Saracen before stomping away.

"What do you think about him?" I asked Saracen.

"He looks guilty. You need to check his alibi."

I nodded. "Is everything okay with you?" Saracen had a sheen of sweat on his forehead.

"Sure. Just fine."

"Wait out here in the shade and cool down. I'll go back in the pub and ask Elspeth if Ricky was hitting on her the afternoon of Pete's murder."

Saracen simply nodded in response.

I hurried back into the pub and caught Elspeth's attention as she served a customer.

"Hey, Holly," she said. "What will it be?"

"No time for a drink. I wanted to see if you remembered a guy hitting on you during the afternoon of the food fair. Were you here?"

She laughed. "All day. And when you're as gorgeous as me, you get hit on all the time. Although they're usually only after a free drink and not this splendid body. Give me his description."

"He was just in here," I said. "Dark hair, leather jacket, stubble. A bit scruffy, but handsome in his own way."

"I remember him," she said. "He called himself Ricky. There's a guy who doesn't like taking no for an answer. He figured himself as some kind of hotshot and must have used a dozen chat up lines. He was kind of amusing for the first half an hour, but it got boring. I shut him down. He stayed by the bar and hung out, dropping a line or two now and again to see if he could soften me up."

"What time did he arrive?"

"I can't say for certain, but it was around three o'clock. It wasn't that busy, and I notice when a new face comes in."

"What time did he leave?"

"He was here until about seven in the evening. Why do you ask?"

"I'm just checking something out," I said as I pushed away from the bar. "Thanks."

"Next time, buy a drink," she said. "Information's not free around here."

"I'll get a double." I gave her a quick wave and headed out the door.

Saracen was sitting on a bench, his head in his hands.

I hurried over to him. "Ricky's alibi checks out. It wasn't him."

He sucked in a breath and nodded.

I sat next to him. "Are you sure you're okay? If you're not feeling well, we can do this another day."

"I feel perfect." He rolled his shoulders and swiped the sweat off his head. "What next?"

"We move on to Dennis Lambeth," I said. "If Ricky's telling the truth, Pete and Dennis got into a fight. Maybe Dennis was out for revenge. He could have crept up on Pete and decided to finish the job. And it makes sense when I think about it. When I saw the body, there were several of Pete's pies smashed around him. That makes this killing personal. Someone hated what Pete did. Dennis fits that perfectly."

"And Pete was putting Dennis's business at risk," Saracen said. "He decided to put a stop to that."

It was looking more likely that Dennis was now in the frame for this.

All we needed to do was find him and get him to talk.

Chapter 11

I tried back in the pub to see if anyone had seen Dennis, but there was no sign of him.

There were only two streets that had stores in Audley St. Mary, and we checked them all and asked the owners if they'd seen Dennis.

He'd been seen around the village first thing this morning, but there were no recent sightings of him.

I entered the lobby of Audley Hotel and went to the reception desk.

Bella Aldrin stood behind it and nodded a greeting when she saw me. "Can I help you with something?"

"I'm trying to find out if you've got a Dennis Lambeth staying here," I said. "I need to ask him some questions."

"Questions about what? We don't usually give out guests' details."

I didn't know Bella well and wasn't certain if bribing her with cake to get information would work. "I don't need to know which room he's in, I just want to know if he's staying here."

"That should be okay. Let me check." She typed information into the computer in front of her before nodding. "He has a room here."

"Can you call his room and see if he's available?"

"No can do. There's a do not disturb message on his line. And I've not seen him all day. He didn't come down for the complimentary breakfast, and I haven't seen him walk through the lobby, but I've not been here all day. Is it urgent? You can leave a message with me. If I see him when he comes down, I can pass it on."

It was strange that Dennis was hiding. It suggested he had a reason to keep a low profile.

I wrote down my phone number and name. "Can you pass this to him? I'd like to talk to him. It's very important."

"Will do."

A commotion outside had me turning. A small crowd had gathered around something on the ground.

I hurried outside to take a look. As I pushed through the crowd, my eyes widened. Saracen lay flat out on his back, his arms splayed out around him.

Jenny Delaney, a local resident, stood in the crowd. "Don't say you've hit someone else with your bike, Holly."

"I was nowhere near him. And the bike's at the castle. Did anyone see what happened? Did he get hit by something?"

"I saw," a woman with bright red hair said. "He sort of swayed a bit and fell backward. No one was near him when it happened."

I knelt beside him. "Saracen! Are you okay?"

He didn't respond. His skin was pale and clammy, and his forehead was dripping with sweat.

I'd exhausted Saracen. I'd dragged him around for hours trying to interview suspects and hadn't looked after him. I shook my head as I felt how rapid his pulse was. He was a grown man; he could have said if he needed to take a break.

"What's wrong with him?" a man in the crowd asked.

"I'm not sure," I said. "I thought he looked a bit pale earlier, but he said he was fine."

"He's got too many layers on," the red-haired woman said. "You need to get that shirt open."

My fingers hovered over the buttons, but Saracen wouldn't want his no doubt fine physique exposed to the tourists visiting Audley St. Mary.

"Has anyone called for an ambulance?" Jenny said.

The crowd murmured, but no one came forward.

I tapped Saracen's cheek lightly, but he didn't respond.

I'd just pulled out my phone to get help, when he sat upright with a groan, his eyes flashing around the crowd.

Saracen leaped up and raised his fists as if expecting trouble.

I jumped in front of him and held my hands up. "There's no need to panic. Nothing bad happened. You don't need to fight anyone."

He grunted, his tight gaze darting around. "What was I doing on the ground?"

"I, um, well, I think you just fainted."

His gaze shot to me and his eyes narrowed. "I never faint."

"There's a first time for everything," I said, hoping I wouldn't have to dodge those enormous fists looming in front of me.

"What are all these people doing here?" he asked.

"Trying to help," I said.

He lowered his fists, swayed from side to side, and fainted again.

Something was terribly wrong with Saracen. Rather than phoning for an ambulance which could take a while to arrive, I dialed Rupert's number.

"Hello?"

"Rupert, it's Holly. I need your help."

"Holly! Whatever's the matter?"

"It's Saracen. He keeps fainting. Any chance you can bring the family doctor into the village? I can't move Saracen. He's splayed out on the ground outside the hotel."

"Is he sick?"

"He must be unwell. Please hurry."

"Of course. We'll be right there."

I shoved my phone back in my pocket and looked around at the growing crowd. "Someone get water and something comfortable for him to rest his head on. It's probably best we don't move him."

"I'd like to see you try," a man said as he stared down at Saracen as if he was an interesting historical relic to be studied.

Several people dashed into the hotel and came back with bottles of water and folded towels, one of which I carefully placed under Saracen's head.

"Maybe it's the flu," someone in the crowd suggested. "He looks like he's running a temperature."

I splashed water on a towel and dabbed his forehead. He was very hot.

"He's overheating," the redhead said. "I really think you should take his clothes off."

I compromised by shrugging him out of his jacket and pushing his sleeves up.

It only seemed like a few minutes had passed before a black SUV screeched to a stop beside us. The crowd parted, and Doctor Michael Evesham and Rupert appeared.

The crowd murmured their surprise at seeing Lord Rupert, but he barely noticed them, his focus on Saracen.

The doctor nodded at me before kneeling next to Saracen. A tall lean man in a black suit and sunglasses also appeared out of the SUV and did an excellent job of crowd control, dispersing everyone in a matter of seconds. I'd seen him around the castle a few times, but we'd never spoken. He was called something like Drayton or Dravel.

"What's wrong with Saracen?" I asked Doctor Evesham.

Doctor Evesham was an attractive middle-aged guy with shoulder-length dark hair. "I suspect he's not managing his condition."

"Condition?" My eyebrows shot up. "He's sick?"

The doctor lifted his arm, inspected his wrist, and tutted. "I knew he wouldn't wear it."

"What's he supposed to wear?" I asked.

"His alert bracelet."

"What does the bracelet alert people to?"

"If Saracen insists on hiding his condition, I'm not at liberty to tell you." He shook his head. "I suggested he use it until he got things stable, but, of course, he didn't want to tarnish the tough-guy image."

I bit my bottom lip. "Is there anything you can do?"

"Of course. He'll soon wake up."

"Is he always going to have this ... problem?"

"Not with the right diet and medication. I've even had some patients who've completely reversed this condition. You can live with it easily as long as you're sensible and don't overindulge in the things you shouldn't."

Rupert took my arm and helped me to stand. We stood back as Doctor Evesham treated Saracen.

"Did you find him like this?" Rupert asked.

"Yes. He was waiting for me while I was asking questions about suspects in Pete's murder," I said. "I kept thinking that he wasn't looking too good, but he insisted there was nothing wrong."

Saracen groaned, and his eyes opened. For a second, he looked alarmed, then let out a sigh when he saw Doctor Evesham.

"I warned you something like this would happen," the doctor said.

"I've been feeling fine," Saracen said. "All of a sudden, I felt woozy and hot."

"Because you haven't been following the diet I recommended," Doctor Evesham said. "You can only play this game so long before something breaks. Let's get you back to the castle. Then we're going to have a long talk about your health and whether I should recommend you take a leave of absence from your position."

Saracen grunted but allowed Doctor Evesham to help him to his feet and guide him toward the SUV.

He looked over at me and ducked his head. "I didn't mean for this to happen."

"Of course you didn't," I said. "If I'd have known you were unwell, I'd have taken better care of you."

His top lip curled. "I'm not an invalid."

"Enough stalling," Doctor Evesham said. "I want to hear all about how you think you're the only person who can cure yourself without the right intervention."

Saracen sighed. He pulled the SUV keys out of his pocket.

"No driving." Doctor Evesham plucked them from his hand.

He scowled at the doctor.

"I can drive the SUV back," Rupert said.

"Good idea." Doctor Evesham handed him the keys.

We headed in a small convoy back to the castle. I went with Rupert while everyone else went in the SUV with Saracen.

"Do you know what's wrong with Saracen?" I asked him.

"No clue. He looks ghastly, though. Really pale and sweaty. I hope it's not contagious. I don't want you to get sick."

"From what Doctor Evesham alluded to it's nothing catching." I still wanted to know what had gone wrong.

Once we arrived back at the castle, I hurried out of the SUV and followed the doctor as he led Saracen to his private apartment in the same complex as mine.

I walked in without an invitation and stood with Rupert as we waited to see how Saracen was doing.

Doctor Evesham came out of Saracen's bedroom and closed the door behind him. "There's nothing to worry about. He'll be fine. I think the worst thing that's been damaged is his ego."

"Is it okay to talk to him?" I asked.

"After the tongue lashing I've given him, I'm sure he'll appreciate a friendly face," Doctor Evesham said.

"I'll show you out." Rupert led him to the door.

"Thanks for coming so quickly," I said.

"That's what I'm here for," Doctor Evesham said.

Rupert returned a moment later. "Shall I come with you to see Saracen?"

"I'll speak to him on my own to begin with," I said. "He must be feeling embarrassed that you saw him collapsed on the ground. He's supposed to be your protector."

"I won't hold that against him," Rupert said. "Give him my best and tell him not to worry about a thing. I'll leave you to it."

I waited until he'd gone, before knocking on the bedroom door and pushing it open.

Saracen sat on his bed, his shoes off and his white shirt untucked. He glanced at me and looked away. "I really screwed the pooch on this one."

I settled on the end of the bed and smiled at him. "Do you want to tell me what's wrong with you? Doctor Evesham was tight-lipped, so I'm none the wiser."

He sighed and pulled at a loose cotton thread on his cuff. "Diabetes."

"Oh my goodness!" I clamped a hand over my mouth. "And I've been feeding you all that cake."

"I could have said no."

"I feel terrible. I made you sick."

"It wasn't your fault. I was being stubborn. I thought the diagnosis was wrong."

I shook my head. "It seems you've got a sweet tooth that's as bad as Campbell's."

"Probably worse," Saracen said. "I didn't want to admit I had a problem. There's a history of diabetes in my family, but I work out and I'm in good shape. I figured I'd be fine. It turns out, I was wrong. And what a way to reveal that to the world."

"Did you have any symptoms before you fainted?"

He shrugged. "I may have done. Actually, I was feeling lousy. I knew the symptoms, but I thought I could fight through them."

"You should have said something to me," I said. "What do I need to do if this happens again?"

"There's not a chance of that. The doctor's just ordered loads more tests and put me on bed rest until my blood sugar is stable."

"I bet you're going to love that," I said.

"It's my own stupid fault."

"But you'll be okay?" I asked.

"So long as I keep away from all your delicious food and cut out the alcohol. The doctor reckons I'll be fine. He even talked about some new diet they're trialing that reverses type two diabetes. It sounds intense, but I'm willing to give it a go if I can get rid of this condition."

"If you need any help with recipes, just let me know," I said. "Does the condition usually get this bad so quickly?"

"Again, that's my fault. I knew something was wrong and deliberately skipped my last check-up a month ago."

"That maybe wasn't the smartest thing to do," I said.

"Yeah, I'm known for my biceps, not my brains."

I smiled at him. "I think you have an excellent brain."

He grinned, but it slid from his face. "Holly, I can't lose my job. I love what I do. Please don't tell Campbell. Hands up, I lied on my last review. I said I had no new medical conditions. He won't let me work for him if he knows I'm sick."

"Saracen, you're great at what you do. You terrify the life out of me the way you skulk around the castle and protect the family. This doesn't need to stop you from doing your job and doing it really well."

His shoulders slumped. "What if Campbell doesn't think that? I could be out of a job. Who'd want to hire me?"

"A lot of people," I said. "There was one determined woman in the crowd when you fainted who wanted to see you without your clothes on. If all else fails, you could get a well-paid job as a naked butler."

He snorted a laugh. "If it comes to that, I'm turning up my heels and going out using death by doughnuts."

"Let's hope it doesn't get that far. Listen, I'm not going to say anything to Campbell, but I think you should. He'll understand, but you need to be honest with him. And if the doctor's right, you can get your blood sugar stable and maybe even reverse this condition, and then everything's good."

"Yeah, I should come clean. I'm really sorry, Holly, but I won't be able to help out with any more of this investigation. You'll have to do this on your own."

I blinked and nodded. It wasn't ideal, but that was just the way it had to be. Campbell was away dealing with an emergency, and Saracen was too sick to help. There was no way I'd force him out of bed to be my sidekick. Or was I his sidekick?

I pulled back my shoulders. "Don't worry. I'll figure out who killed Pete. And when I do, we can celebrate the victory together."

"With some no sugar, tasteless dessert."

I chuckled and shook my head. "I'm sure I can do better than that."

Chapter 12

I was up early the next morning and scrolling through the internet, researching type two diabetes. There was a wealth of information online, and I was amazed to read that Doctor Evesham was right. There was an opportunity to reverse the condition with the right diet.

I'd also discovered dozens of amazing recipes that I planned to use to make delicious meals for Saracen. If I could do anything to help him get better, I would.

With my new recipes in hand, I grabbed Meatball his breakfast, settled him in his kennel, then hurried to the kitchen and whipped up two high-protein, smoked salmon omelettes. I'd join Saracen for his first meal to beat his condition.

I carried the plates to his apartment and knocked on the door.

It took a while, but he finally answered. His face was a picture of misery.

I held up the omelettes. "Rough night?"

He stepped aside and let me in. "I did a lot of thinking in the small hours. I've been dumb. I let my sweet tooth get the better of me."

"Well, I take that as a huge compliment. You couldn't resist my amazing desserts, despite knowing they'd make you unwell." I set the omelettes on the table. "You'll be pleased to learn there are lots of tasty recipes you can still enjoy while you're getting your condition under control. You're not going to miss out."

"No triple chocolate fudge brownies with sugar sprinkles and chocolate dipped hazelnuts on top, though?" He stared at the omelettes.

My nose wrinkled as I shook my head. "We'll find a workaround. And I figured since you're out of active commission, I can still use that brainpower of yours to talk through the suspects."

"I'm happy to help." He gestured to the table. "Do you want a coffee with that?"

"That would be great." I settled in a seat, and Saracen joined me a moment later with two steaming mugs of coffee.

"I wanted to say thanks for yesterday," he said. "You could have told Campbell everything. I wouldn't have blamed you if you had."

"It's not my secret to tell," I said.

He dug into his omelette. "This is really good."

"I do know a thing or two about cooking."

"Ain't gonna argue with that. Campbell's a decent boss. He's tough but fair. He demands the best from his team. I guess that's why I was so hesitant about telling him about my diabetes. I didn't want to look weak in his eyes."

"Did you know Campbell before you joined the security team?" I asked.

"Our paths crossed a few times. We both served in the SAS. We were in separate squads sent on Operation Blade."

"What's that?"

He arched an eyebrow. "Top secret. Ever heard of Operation Barras in Sierra Leone?"

"Nope. Another secret mission?"

"Not so secret anymore. Operation Barras was basically a hostage situation that went wrong. Our mission was almost identical. We were sent in to stop the local military creating chaos. We got in, killed the bad guys, and rescued the good guys. Job done."

I blew out a breath. Once Saracen opened up, he really opened up. "That's impressively terrifying."

"That's me." He grinned and ate more omelette.

"That's how you came to know Campbell and his petrifyingly awesome skills?"

"Yeah, but don't let him know I've been telling you about his past. He went on to bigger and better things after that. Campbell worked at the very top with some important people."

"And now he guards the Audley family," I said. "Is that a promotion or a demotion?"

"Neither. He decided he'd seen enough of the front line. He put his life at risk all the time. He calls this his semi-retirement, but don't let anyone else know that either, or you might just disappear one night and never be seen again. The pay's great, the work's generally easy, and he's got full control."

"Campbell does seem to have a lot of control around here," I said. "Including the investigations that take place on the estate."

"That's not Campbell's influence. It's historical privilege, and an amiable police force in the village whose budget keeps getting cut."

"Of course, I should have thought of that. I did some work on historical privilege during my history degree."

"You studied history?"

I waggled a finger in the air. "I did. And I remember that historical privilege is all about a landowner forming an agreement to manage crimes on their property."

"That's it. The agreement dates back hundreds of years. It was a different set up then, there weren't even real police around, so it made sense for the Audleys to manage things. The agreement still stands, and the local police don't mind. We don't exclude them. I get the impression they're glad to have an extra few pairs of hands. They've been briefed on the security team backgrounds and know we're not out to cause trouble. Have you met the guy who runs the police around here?"

"Nope. I've not had anything to do with him," I said.

"Nor will you, unless you play golf. Dudley Fabin's on the road to retirement. He's been that way ever since he joined as Chief of Police. He spends most of his time playing golf and the rest of it shoving paperwork onto other people. He was happy to hand over responsibility about any crimes on the estate, providing we keep him informed. It's a win-win all around. Campbell likes to be in control of a situation."

"Yes, I'd noticed that."

Saracen grinned. "He only comes down hard on people because he expects the very best from them." The grin vanished. "And I haven't given that. I've hidden things from him. I'm not sure I'm coming back from this."

"You will. You've been helpful, not just as my cake tester, but in this investigation."

"I won't be testing any more of your delicious cakes." He blew out a breath and stabbed at his omelette. "You know, I figured you for a cake girl through and through, not a history buff as well."

"Cakes and corsets, that's me," I said. "Baking was always a passion, but I also had this wild ambition to research and write amazing non-fiction books about British history. The trouble is, I can't write for toffee. I had a few goes, but it was all over the place. So, I turned to my second love. After my history degree, I did two years in a catering college and worked part time in a couple of cafés to get lots of hands-on experience."

"You're perfect as a baker. I'm gutted I won't be able to enjoy your food."

"Sure you will." I pointed my knife at his omelette. "It will just get better. You can be my experiment."

He grunted. "I'm not sure what I think about that."

"You won't feel any pain, and you'll get to try lots of delicious experiments. How does that sound?"

"Hmmm. Not bad."

"Perfect. And we can still figure out this murder together. The next step is to find Dennis. I was wondering if he had something to do with Pete's missing laptop. The fact it was there when Pete was alive and gone once he'd been murdered suggests there's a connection. Whoever has the laptop could be the killer."

"Let's track it," Saracen said.

"I'll get out my super spy laptop detecting kit, shall I?"

"Funny girl. If you've got the IP address, we can find the location of the laptop."

"How do we get that?"

"We need Pete's email address. That should be linked to the laptop. I can make a call if you like. We've got access to a team of super geeks who operate offsite. They do just this sort of thing."

Why wasn't I surprised to hear that? "Before you do, there might be someone closer to home who has the information we need. Maisie did all sorts of work for Pete. She must know his email address."

"Good thinking."

"You stay here and finish your breakfast. I'll speak to Maisie and see if she can help us."

He nodded as he cut off a large piece of omelette. "Thanks again, Holly. For the food, and for, well, everything."

"Any time." I left him to his food and hurried over to the vendors' parking lot. I walked over to the open back door of Pete's truck and poked my head inside. Maisie was there, studying six pies sitting on a shelf.

She glanced over and smiled. "Morning, Holly."

"Hard at work?" I asked.

"I'm wondering which one of these to use for the contest. Did you hear, I got through to the finals?"

"That's great news," I said. "Same here."

"Oh no! I've tried your cakes. They're amazing. You'll be hard to beat."

"There'll be an overall winner, but there are also commendations and smaller prizes for other entrants. I'm not guaranteed a win."

"You sound like you know you're going to win. Don't tell me you're pulling strings from inside the castle?"

I tried not to feel affronted. "My food speaks for itself. Besides, the final taste test will be done blind. The judges will have no idea who's made what. It's a level playing field."

She shrugged. "That sounds fair. Is there something I can do for you?"

"This might sound a bit strange, but can you tell me what Pete's email address is?"

"Of course. I use it all the time. Actually, I even have his password. He was always getting me to reply to people about orders or deliveries that needed to be arranged. Is there something you need to see on his emails?"

"If you wouldn't mind me having a look, that would be great, but I'm mainly after his email address."

"Do you think there's something in the emails connected to his murder?" She flipped open the netbook on the counter and tapped on the keyboard.

"There might be, but I'm also interested in tracing his missing laptop. We can track it based on his email."

"You don't say? Okay, here's his email. He gets a lot of inappropriate emails so skim past those. Some of the jokes his friends send him are filthy. From a brief look, there's nothing strange in here. How quickly can you track the laptop?" She moved to the side, and I had a look through Pete's emails. There was nothing that stood out as odd.

"I imagine it'll be instantaneous. Honestly, I've no clue how it works. The castle security does some kind of magic to track things that go missing."

"Will the laptop need to be turned on?"

"I'm not sure. Maybe." I stepped back. "Have you got a pen and paper? I'll take down Pete's email."

"Sure." She handed me what I needed, and I scribbled down the information. "Let me know if you hear anything. It's weird Pete not being around. Much quieter, though. He was always shouting orders. I'd gotten used to it. It's sort of nice now to do my own work and not chase around after him all the time."

"Do you think you'll stay in the catering business now he's gone?"

"Absolutely. Although my days on a food truck and racing from one food fair to another are over. Now I've got experience, I might look around for a sous chef position in a restaurant."

"Good luck with that," I said. "And thanks for letting me look at the emails."

"I just hope it helps."

"Me too." I waved her goodbye and hurried back to Saracen's apartment with the information he needed.

He'd washed up our plates and mugs and was pacing around the lounge as I entered. "You got it?"

"I did." I passed him the information.

Saracen settled in front of his own laptop. "Let's see what we can find."

"You can track it from here?"

"Of course. The complicated stuff is left to the real tech geeks, but we're trained in how to track people. It can come in useful during kidnappings, or when people go missing. Our VIPs like to escape our notice. Some of them have embarrassing hobbies they don't like us to see. Real kinky stuff, sometimes."

"Huh! Tell me more," I said.

"I'd love to, but then I'd have to kill you."

I was pretty sure he wasn't joking.

After a few minutes of tapping information on the keyboard and running through searches, Saracen slapped a hand on the table. "We've got it. It's a Lenovo Model S12."

"Where is it?"

"The laptop's still in the village."

I stared at the pulsing red dot on the screen. "That's not far from here. It's maybe twenty minutes away. I should go take a look."

Saracen scrubbed his chin. "It's not safe for you to go out and find it on your own. The killer could still have it."

That was true, and it was a concern, but if I found this laptop, it could lead us to the killer. The answer was almost within my grasp.

"I'll take a quick look," I said. "I'll be careful. If there's any sign of danger, I'll back off and get help."

"I could always come with you," Saracen said.

"Absolutely not. You're under the doctor's orders to rest. You don't want the stress of going hunting for this laptop. It might mess up your blood sugar again. How about I do a little recon mission? I won't go in anywhere alone; I'll just take a look around. Maybe the laptop was stolen and dumped in a ditch. I might find it on the side of the road smashed beyond repair. That would solve this particular mystery."

"I'm not happy about this," Saracen said. "Don't put yourself at risk."

"We've almost got the killer," I said. "I'll be on my best behavior, but we can't waste any time. I'll take a look and report back to you."

"Do that. But be careful. If you wind up dead on my watch, Campbell really will fire me."

"I'll try not to die. I wouldn't want that on your conscience."

"Holly! I'm not joking about this. Be sensible."

I grinned as I headed to the door. "I'll stay out of trouble."

As I headed away from Saracen's apartment, I uncrossed my fingers. I felt a bit guilty for not telling him the complete truth, but we were so close to solving this. Find the laptop, find the killer. If I had to face a little danger while that happened, then so be it.

Chapter 13

I decided to use my delivery bike to get to the location of the laptop. The IP address showed that it was on Threadneedle Lane. It was a narrow road, and you could just about squeeze one car along it until you got to the end where it widened out. It might take me a bit longer to get there, but the bike was more discreet. I could sneak about more easily than I could in a noisy vehicle.

"Woof woof." Meatball bounced out of his kennel when he spotted me and wagged his tail.

"It's best you stay here, boy. This could be dangerous."

"Woof." His tail drooped.

"I'll make it up to you with a big lunch."

He turned away and stomped into his kennel.

"Stop right there!" Alice appeared, her cheeks red as she gasped in air.

"What's going on?" I asked.

"I've just been with Granny. She told me that there's a high chance you're about to die."

I blinked rapidly, and my mouth went dry. "Another one of her predictions?"

"And you know how good they are. I'm not leaving your side. I'll protect you."

I climbed off the bike and walked closer. "Exactly how are you going to do that?"

"Prop the bike up," Alice said.

I leaned the bike against the wall. "Why? What are you going to—"

She grabbed my arm, flung her weight against me, and flipped me over her shoulder. I landed on my back, staring at the sky in a stunned silence.

Meatball launched himself out of his kennel. "Woof, woof, woof, woof, woooooof."

"Your mommy is fine. I'd never hurt her." Alice stepped over me and grinned. "Impressed?"

"I'm okay, Meatball." I gestured at him to stop barking and sucked in a breath. "What just happened?"

She giggled as she held out her hand and pulled me to my feet. "We're trained to protect ourselves. It's in case we ever get kidnapped by some underhand sort. I'm a green belt in tae kwon do."

"How did I not know about this?"

She pressed a finger to her lips. "It's top secret. If anyone comes after us, we need to appear as if we can't look after ourselves. It puts them on the back foot and they lower their guard. That's when I'd strike. Take them out with a sucker punch and run for it. Well, I'd try running away. That's one thing I've never been good at. Oh, that and drawing, sewing, playing the piano, and singing. And dancing. Other than that, I've got some killer moves."

"I'm not going to disagree with that." I brushed mud off the back of my pants. "Okay, you're my backup."

"Excellent. I'll go grab the tandem bike."

"Tandem what now?"

"It's much more fun when you ride in tandem. There's even a basket on the front for Meatball." She petted his head as he bounded around us, checking I was okay after Alice's surprise attack.

I pinched the bridge of my nose as Alice bounced away. This recon mission had just gotten complicated.

Alice wheeled out a huge bright pink bike with a large basket on the front. "You get on the front, and I'll do the back."

I'd never ridden a tandem bike. I adjusted the seat and hopped on. It felt a lot heavier than my usual bike.

"Meatball must come too," Alice said.

"Woof woof." He wagged his tail and danced on his back legs.

"Okay, he can be extra backup." I raced to my apartment, grabbed our helmets, and hurried back, carefully securing Meatball's before placing him in his new basket.

He gave it a good sniff before he turned around and settled, seeming quite happy.

"Ready when you are," Alice said.

I turned to see she'd hitched up her long blue dress and tucked most of it into the waistband. It looked like she was wearing a giant pair of flappy blue knickers. "Are you sure about this?"

"Absolutely. Granny's never wrong. As soon as she told me you were about to leave and your life was in danger, I ran down the stone steps to find you and save you from your doom."

"It's probably only going to be a tiny amount of danger," I said, really not sure I should take a princess into a potentially deadly situation.

"As you've just discovered, I'm ready for danger. What are we waiting for?"

"On three?" I said.

Alice nodded. "One, two, threeeeeeee!"

I pushed off with my foot, and after a wobbly few seconds, we found a rhythm as we cycled through the castle's grounds and onto the public road.

I was soon sweating and pedaling twice as hard as I usually did. A quick glance over my shoulder told me why. Alice wasn't pedaling. "Do you mind giving me a hand, your majesty? This thing is heavy."

"Sorry, I got distracted by the scenery. It's been ages since I've been out on a bike. What fun."

"It would be even more fun if I wasn't doing all the work."

"I'm pedaling now!"

"Only sometimes," I mumbled. I was glad we'd reached the top of the first hill, and I got to slack off as we rode down. "We're heading to Threadneedle Lane."

"I know," she said. "Granny said that's where you'd be going."

"How can she be so accurate about this particular prediction?"

"When someone she cares about is in mortal peril, her visions become clearer."

"She should work for Campbell if she's that good," I said.

"Maybe she already does." Alice giggled. "Oh bother! We've got company behind us. I'd thought I'd given them the slip."

I glanced over my shoulder again to see a large black SUV following us. "I hope they don't get too close or they'll give us away."

Alice waved a hand at the SUV. "They know not to get too near."

I stopped pedaling. "Since they're here, why can't we grab a ride with them?"

"No, silly! You don't want to scare off the killer. If we turn up looking all menacing with our private security in tow that could spoil it all. The killer will make a run for it before I karate chop them."

"We don't want an easy ride, do we? And I thought you did tae kwon do, not karate?"

"I do both. So, fill me in. Why are we going to Threadneedle Lane? Will the killer really be there?"

"Hopefully not. We're looking for Pete's missing laptop," I said. "We traced its location. Well, Saracen did."

"There isn't much along that lane," Alice said. "A couple of cottages at the first turn, but then it leads to the recycling center."

I sucked in a breath. "Of course! What better place to hide a laptop?"

"Yuck! Don't tell me we're going to search everybody's trash for this missing laptop?"

"I wouldn't dream of asking you to do something so base, Princess," I said.

"Just so you know, I am sticking my tongue out at you," she said.

I chuckled. "This is a clever move by whoever took the laptop. The recycling center deals with all kinds of materials. It's a perfect hiding place."

We turned into Threadneedle Lane and cycled along until we reached the entrance of the recycling center.

I stopped the bike and leaned to one side, resting my foot on the ground. My gaze ran over the half a dozen huge metal containers of recycling. If the laptop was in here, there was no way we were going to find it.

Alice hopped off the bike and hurried to the front. "What are you waiting for?"

"I'm trying to get over the overwhelming sense of defeat that covered me when I looked at all that recycling."

"How about you start with the electricals?"

That wasn't a bad idea. Maybe our killer was green-minded. "What are you going to do?"

"It looks strange if we come to a recycling center and have nothing to recycle. I'm going to sweet talk the staff.

This can be an unplanned visit to show our appreciation of their hard work in keeping our village beautiful and free of trash. While I get the foreman to show me around this wonderful, pungent smelling site, you head to those big cages of electricals and see if the laptop's in there."

I'd thought it before, but Alice was so much more than the blonde bimbo she pretended she was.

"That's an excellent plan."

Alice giggled. "Come on, it's show time." She turned and smiled sweetly at the large, bald man wearing a fluorescent jacket who was staring at her in shock.

"Princess Alice?" he stammered.

"The one and only. Unless you count Queen Victoria's child, Alice. But of course, she's dead. Apparently, she was lovely. A big supporter of women's causes. I'm certain she would have loved to visit a place like this." She strode over, took hold of his arm, and turned him away from me. "I hope you don't mind me taking up your valuable time. I'd like to look around. I was saying to the Duchess the other day what amazing work you do."

"Oh! Well, that's good of you, Princess. You really want to take a look around?" His gaze ran over her silk dress and white shoes. "It's not the cleanest of places."

"I'll be fine. I can brush any dirt off my clothes. I'm really interested in your scrap metal. Why don't we start with that?" She led him to the farthest end of the recycling center, giving me a discreet thumbs up behind her back as she walked away.

Several other workers on site trailed behind them as if they couldn't believe what they were seeing.

I grinned as I pushed my bike through the center and headed toward the cages housing the electrical items. There were five large metal containers, packed full of ancient rusting microwaves, lime-scaled kettles, several bulky computer screens, and broken blenders. I glanced around to make sure no one was looking before starting the hunt for the laptop.

"Woof woof." Meatball bounced up and down in the basket.

"I'll let you out, but you have to stay on your leash," I said. "There's lots of machinery around here, including things that crush adorable little pups because they can't see them. I don't want you anywhere near those."

"Woof."

"That's right. No messing with the dangerous equipment." I lifted him out of the basket, made sure his extendable leash was secured, and then wrapped it around my wrist before continuing my search.

I found a couple of laptops, but neither was the right model.

The leash tugged around my wrist, and I turned, gently tugging back to let Meatball know he'd gone as far as he was allowed.

The leash slackened as he returned. He sat by my feet and dropped a filthy old boot next to me.

"Good effort, but no juicy bone for you. We're looking for a laptop."

"Woof woof." He bounced away again, his tail wagging with delight.

I found another two laptops, both the wrong kind.

I moved onto the final cage of electricals. There was no guarantee that whoever took the laptop put it here. They could have tossed it inside any of these recycling containers to hide the evidence.

Meatball returned again. This time, he had three grubby tennis balls stuffed into his mouth. He dropped each one on the ground and grinned up at me.

"You're very clever for finding those," I said. "They're so much nicer than the dozens of clean, sweet smelling toys you've got back home."

"Woof woof." He bounced away again.

He made two more trips and arrived back with two more equally disgusting balls.

"Hey! What are you doing over here?" A tall broad man with a scruffy beard strode over to me.

Meatball growled and guarded his newfound tennis balls.

"Oh! Nothing. I was just checking to see—"

"And here we are at the electricals." Alice emerged on the other side of the metal cages, still holding tightly to the foreman's arm. "It's all been so fascinating. What do you do with these?" She raised her eyebrows and nodded at me.

The man who'd found me poking around was still glaring, but uncertainty crossed his face as he witnessed a beautiful silk clad princess emerge from the trash.

"Holly! There you are," Alice said. "I hope you're finding the visit useful. Holly's my assistant. She comes everywhere with me. She's very industrious, but a bit obsessed with computers. You couldn't resist this lot, could you?" She gave me a discreet wink.

"It's all very interesting," I said.

The bearded man who'd accosted me seemed to have forgotten I existed as he stared at Alice.

"Everyone's working so hard," she said. "When I get back to the castle, I'll make sure the Duchess sends you some thank you gifts for your efforts in keeping our lovely village so clean and green."

"That's very good of you, Princess," the foreman said. "There's really no need. We're just doing our jobs."

"Although some treats would be nice," the bearded man said.

Alice giggled. "Then it's all arranged. Well, have we seen everything we need to?" She addressed the question to me.

The laptop wasn't in the cages, and the place was too big to search on our own. "We have. Thanks for letting us look around."

"Any time you want to come back, you just let me know," the foreman said. "It's been a pleasure to show you around."

"The pleasure has been all mine." Alice let go of his arm, caught hold of mine, and we hurried away as I pushed the bike alongside me.

Meatball trotted along beside us, his mouth full of the manky tennis balls he'd collected.

"Any sign of the laptop?" she whispered.

"No. It could be anywhere in here. The killer obviously wasn't green-minded, and we can't hunt through all this trash."

Alice slowed as we reached the exit. "What we need is a pie."

I stared at her. "What are you talking about?"

"We need something to eat. Something to stimulate the old gray matter and help us figure this out."

"Okay, but I've not long had breakfast. Why do you want a pie in particular?"

"Because I've just spotted that food truck over there covered in pictures of pies."

I followed the direction her finger was pointing, and my mouth fell open. I slapped the side of my head. "I've been such an idiot. I didn't even see that when we rode past. That's Dennis's food truck. We've been looking in the wrong place."

Chapter 14

We hurried over to the food truck. I rested the bike against the side of it before peeping in through the window.

"Is Dennis in there?" Alice whispered.

"There's no sign of anyone inside," I said.

"Come look. The door's open."

I hurried around the side and saw her grasping the handle. "Isn't that breaking and entering?"

"No! I've seen the TV shows. If there's a just cause and impediment to go inside the premises, then it's not breaking any laws."

"You're getting marriage vows mixed up with the police right of entry," I said.

"It's the same thing," she said. "It's all legal and binding. The door's unlocked, which means it's fine to go in and have a friendly chat with our neighborhood killer. And if he's not there, we might just accidentally look around and find something incriminating while we wait for him."

"Keep your voice down," I said. "He might be asleep in there, and I missed him."

"If anything gets serious, we have backup." She pointed over my shoulder at the black SUV lingering by the curb.

"We can take a quick look," I said. "The first sign of trouble, we're out of here."

"You sound almost as serious as Campbell," she said.

"He has sort of put me in charge."

"I heard you were his secretary, going around taking notes and typing up the dictation."

I scowled at her. "I'm definitely not Campbell's secretary. It was a case of desperate times called for desperate measures, and I was the only option he had. Anyway, get in the food truck before people notice us poking around and call the police."

Alice stepped inside and wrinkled her nose. "It smells like gone off cheese in here."

I crept in after her with Meatball and had a quick look inside one of the refrigerators. "That's because there are several blocks of stinking blue Stilton cheese in here."

"That's it! I knew I could smell something nasty. I don't mind a bit of brie, but that's about as strong as I go. Men are obsessed with their strong smelling moldy cheeses."

"Let's concentrate on finding the laptop and not worrying about the stinky cheese." I closed the refrigerator door and cast my gaze around the food truck. It was a standard layout, with a large food preparation area along one side, shelves with condiments lining them, two large refrigerators, and a freezer for food storage. The hatch to the food truck was shut, so it was gloomy inside.

"Any sign of the laptop?" I whispered.

"I can't see it. I'll take the right side, you take the left. We'll go through the cupboards and find it," Alice said.

I nodded as I got to work on pulling open the sliding drawers and taking a look inside. Everything was neat and orderly, but it was all cooking equipment and utensils.

The laptop had to be in here. Dennis must have taken it after he'd killed Pete and stashed it away. There could be important information on there he needed to keep.

Meatball dropped his dirty tennis balls on the floor of the truck and growled.

I headed to the back door and peered out the small window. My stomach clenched, and I backed away. "Dennis is coming!"

"We need to hide!" Alice bumped against the walls before ducking behind the counter.

"I can still see you," I said. "Your skirt is sticking out."

"What are we going to do?" She stood from her hiding place, her eyes wide.

I swallowed my nerves and stood in front of the door. "Stay behind me."

The door swung open, and Dennis stepped inside. He froze for a second. "What the heck are you doing here?"

"It's so lovely to see you again." Alice brushed past me, a wide smile on her face. "I was just saying to Holly that we had to meet the best pie maker in this country. And here you are."

Indecision raced across his face before it settled into a frown. "What are you talking about? What are you doing in my truck?"

"Waiting for you," Alice said. "We were hoping to get treats from you before you left the village. Please say we can buy some of your lovely pies."

His forehead wrinkled as his gaze went from Alice to me. "You were at the food fair. What are you doing here?"

"Just like Princess Alice said, we were hoping to buy some of your produce." It didn't sound like a great lie, no matter how we phrased it.

"I haven't got anything for sale. And this is private property. You'd better not have damaged the door breaking in here." Dennis leaned down and checked the lock.

"Oh, no. We'd never do that." Alice flashed me a puzzled look. For once, her charm wasn't working. "It was open. We thought we'd wait inside until you got back."

His lips pursed, and his gaze ran over the food counter. "I hope you haven't been messing with my equipment. There's expensive stuff in here."

"We haven't touched a thing," Alice said.

"Good. You need to leave." He advanced on us swiftly.

Meatball barked and growled, doing his best impression of a tiny brown wolf.

Alice ducked behind me, and I backed up, my calves bashing into the small seating area. I toppled backward and landed heavily on a seat. As I sat up, there was something hard beneath me. I reached under the cushion and pulled out a laptop.

Alice gasped. "You found it! Is that the missing laptop?"

I grimaced and discreetly shook my head at her. "Is this yours?" I asked Dennis.

"What? No, that's not mine. Why did you put it there?"

"I didn't. Why were you hiding it?" A quick check of the laptop model showed me this was what we'd been looking for.

He stared at the laptop. "I've no clue what you're talking about. I'm telling you, I've never seen that before."

He was lying. He had to be. "Alice, it's time for that backup."

"I'm on it." She leaned out the door and waved frantically.

"What backup are you talking about?" Dennis glared at me. "What mess are you getting me into?"

"I have questions for you about Pete Saunders," I said.

He lifted his hands, palms facing me. "I've answered all the questions and given a statement already. I'm leaving today. You can't stop me."

"I definitely can't," I said. "But this is Pete's missing laptop. Did you take it after you killed him?"

Dennis staggered back, his hand going to his chest. "I didn't kill him."

"You didn't like him," I said.

"I don't like a lot of people. There's always someone trying to undercut me or put me out of business. That doesn't mean I go around killing them." He jabbed a finger at the laptop. "And that's got nothing to do with me. For all I know, you put it there. Maybe you're framing me for this murder."

Two of the castle's security guards appeared in the doorway.

"This man needs to be taken into custody," Alice said. "He's guilty of murdering Pete Saunders."

"No! You've got it all wrong." Dennis backed away from the men.

"There's no need to cause a scene, sir," one of the security guards said. "Come with us."

"I'm not going anywhere with you. You're not the police," Dennis said.

"But they're assisting with the police inquiries into Pete's murder. Surely you want to help with that," I said. "Especially if it clears your name."

"I don't want to help Pete. He caused me nothing but trouble since he set up his business. He runs a shambles of a business. I'm embarrassed to be seen at the same event with him."

"So you killed him," I said. "He made you angry, put your business at risk, and you struck back. Did he say something to provoke you?"

One of the security guards caught hold of Dennis's arm, and after a brief struggle, they pulled him out of the food truck.

"This is insane," Dennis said. "I'm innocent."

I stood with Alice and Meatball as Dennis was marched to the black SUV and shoved inside.

She turned and tightly hugged me. "We did it! We found the murderer. We've cracked the case. Campbell will be so proud of me."

"So proud of us, don't you mean?"

She stepped back. "You know what I mean. This will show him that I can achieve anything."

"And why do you want to impress Campbell so badly?"

She nudged me with her elbow. "Because I want him to think well of me. There's nothing wrong with that." She smoothed her hands over her crumpled silk skirt.

"Of course not. So long as that's all it is, and it's not because you have a little crush on your security guard."

"What crush? I don't know what you're talking about. It's not as if I could marry him. Mommy would never allow it. She'd say he wasn't appropriate."

"You told me once that you'd only ever marry for love. If that's the case, surely status isn't important." I was teasing her, but only gently.

"Stop making things difficult." She smacked me on the back of the arm. "It's time to celebrate."

"Before we do that, why don't we take a look at this laptop and see why it's so important," I said. "Maybe why it was worth killing over."

"Do you think we should? It could be crucial to the investigation."

"Put on a pair of these." I handed her some blue plastic food preparation gloves. "If we wear them, we won't disturb any evidence on the laptop."

"You're so clever, Holly. I'd have been jabbing away at the keys for hours before I even thought about fingerprints. You've clearly watched a lot more TV cop dramas than I have."

I grinned as I opened the laptop carefully. "One or two. Although I like my mysteries in book form. Give me an Agatha Christie and I'm more than happy."

"Oh yes, she's very good."

There was an hour of battery power on the laptop when I fired it up. That would give us enough time to have a look and see what was on here.

I pulled out my phone and called Saracen. "We've got the laptop."

"Good work, Holly. Bring it back here."

"Any chance you can get your cyber geeks to access it remotely? There's a password protecting it, and we can't get in."

There was a pause. "You're not supposed to be tampering with evidence."

"We're wearing gloves," I said. "It's all above board. And, guess where we found the laptop?"

"Exactly where I said it would be?"

I lifted my gaze to the ceiling. "Even better. Dennis Lambeth had it on his food truck. It's parked on Threadneedle Lane. He's the killer."

There was silence for a second. "You were seen leaving the castle with Princess Alice on a tandem bike. Please tell me you didn't get her involved in this."

"Alice is more than capable of looking after herself. I got a first-hand demonstration of just how lethal she can be."

"Even so, I had to pull two men from castle security to go after her."

"You're missing the good news. We found the laptop. Dennis put on a great show of pretending as if he'd never seen it before, but he has to be involved."

A heavy sigh slid down the phone. "Dennis showed up?"

"And he was apprehended by the excellent backup you sent after Princess Alice. The case is almost solved. So, stop telling me off and put me through to your cyber geeks so we can get this thing open and find out what's so important about it."

Saracen grunted. "We're going to have words about this."

"Be angry with me later. Let's find out why Dennis killed Pete."

"Patching you through now." A phone connected and was picked up after five rings.

"Good morning, caller. Your identification has been cleared."

"It has? Oh! Um ... that's good to hear. I'm Holly. What's your name?"

"You don't need my name. Give me the IP address of the laptop."

I wasn't sure how to find that out, but after a few helpful instructions from the mysterious woman on the other end of the line, I discovered it and read it back to her.

"One moment please."

Within seconds, the mouse was moving on its own on the laptop screen.

Alice nudged me, and I shifted over to make room for her as we watched the cyber security expert get to work.

"This is like working with a secret agent," she whispered. "What's that character in the Bond movies called? The one with all the gadgets?"

"Bond has got nothing on us," the woman on the other end of the line said. "This is real life. Things get deadly."

Alice stifled a giggle behind her hand. "She's very serious."

"Saving lives is always a serious business, Princess."

I raised my eyebrows at her and grinned.

"The laptop is now accessible. All files are available to you."

"Thanks for your help," I said. "Where should I send the thank you card to?"

The call disconnected. Being an elusive security geek must mean you had to have a sense of humor bypass.

"Where shall we start?" Alice asked.

"Let's take a look through Pete's files." I skimmed through the files but didn't find anything out of the ordinary. It was a bit of a mess, lots of old invoices stuck on the desktop, nothing in order, and letters from years ago.

"There's nothing exciting in here," Alice said.

"He's hardly going to have a file named 'devious plan to murder Pete Saunders' for us to find. Let's check out his web history. That might be more interesting."

I took a couple of minutes to search back through everything Pete had been looking at over the last month. Again, nothing stuck out as strange.

"He was planning a vacation to Australia," Alice said. "Look, he was checking out flight times and costs."

I scrolled through more of the history. There was nothing there.

An instant message appeared in the corner of the computer screen. I opened it.

You have access to Pete's bank account.

The login details appeared a second later.

"These cyber geeks know what they're doing." I pulled up Pete's bank login page and keyed in the details.

A brief scan of the information showed nothing amiss. Regular money coming in and going out.

"Here's a monthly payment going out to Ricky Stormy. That must be for the loan Pete took out." I tapped my fingers on the table. "Ricky claimed that Pete wasn't paying him back. This shows that wasn't true."

"Why lie about that?" Alice asked.

"Maybe there was a second loan," I said. "Pete might have needed money in an emergency and got in trouble when he couldn't pay it back as quickly as Ricky demanded."

Alice sat back and sighed. "I was hoping something exciting would show up on the laptop. The reason Dennis stole it. Maybe naughty pictures of Dennis with a married woman, or something like that."

I rubbed the end of my nose. I'd been hoping for the same thing. Not the smutty pictures, but a clear reason Dennis felt he had to kill Pete. This wasn't much help. I shut down the laptop and closed the lid.

"Let's take this to the experts. And we need to get back to the castle and grill Dennis about what the laptop was doing in his possession."

Alice clapped her hands together. "How exciting! My first proper interrogation. I can go to the dungeon and get finger clamps."

I glanced at her. She was alarmingly keen to hurt someone. "Let's wait before we use the finger clamps. We can start by asking some simple questions."

"And if he doesn't answer them? Can I bring out the clamps?"

"We'll negotiate on that point." I grabbed the bike and headed over to the SUV with Alice and Meatball.

Sometimes, I wondered about her thirst for all things gruesome. If she wasn't talking about lopping off someone's head, she wanted to use medieval torture devices on suspects.

I knew how to pick some seriously weird friends. But why not? It made my life more interesting.

Alice bounced on her toes and giggled. "Let's get interrogating."

Chapter 15

"We should be in that room asking the questions." Alice stood with her hands on her hips as she stared down the giant security guard who blocked our way.

"This is for your safety, Princess." Kace Delaney stood in front of the closed door his colleague, Mason Sloane, had walked through with Dennis a few moments ago.

"We made the arrest," Alice said. "We must be allowed to interrogate him. Saracen said we could."

"Princess, leave that to us. We've gotten all the information we need from you." Kace cast a worried look at me as if hoping I'd intervene and remove Alice before she caused trouble.

During the short trip back to the castle in the SUV, I'd filled the security guards in on everything we'd discovered. They'd contacted Saracen and updated him. He'd arranged to have Dennis questioned, along with an investigation of the laptop and a search of the food truck. At no point was it suggested that Alice or I could question Dennis.

"I can order you to let us into that room," Alice said. "And why did you take Dennis into the saloon, anyway?

Surely he'd be better in the dungeon. It's where we have all the best torture devices."

Kace cleared his throat. "We'll move the suspect if necessary. Although I'm hoping we won't need to resort to torture to get the answers."

I tugged gently on Alice's sleeve. "Why don't we let them question Dennis for now?"

"Where's the fun in that?" she asked. "We did the hard work, and they get the credit."

"Saracen knows what's going on," I said. "We can always take over if they can't manage." I winked at Kace.

"I suppose we do need to celebrate." Alice's eyes lit up, and she turned to me. "Have you got any of those strawberry scones with that incredible lavender infused fresh cream? I had two yesterday. They were delicious. It's the perfect food to celebrate our victory."

"Of course. Let's head to the kitchen and see what we can find." I was relieved how easy it was to distract Alice. She was happy now fresh cream scones were on the agenda.

"I love your scones. I've never had a nicer one. Even when I went to Cornwall. I tried a dozen different scones on my visit. None of them were a patch on yours."

"That's good to know." We walked alongside each other, heading to the kitchen. "And now Dennis has been caught, I'm out of danger. That's even more reason to celebrate."

"Oh! I can't guarantee that," Alice said. "Granny didn't give me a timeline. Your life could still be at risk."

My heart stuttered. That was reassuring to know.

The kitchen was bustling with lunchtime activity as we walked in. Chef Heston glared at me, but his gaze shifted to Princess Alice.

He shook his head. "Let me guess, you're still on official castle business? I suppose it's too much to ask that you do some work around here today?"

"I'll stay late tonight if anything needs finishing up," I said. "I won't let you down."

"And we must celebrate," Alice said. "We just caught a killer."

Chef Heston's expression morphed into one of disbelief. "Congratulations."

"We'll have scones and tea all round," Alice said. "Everyone's welcome to join us."

"We'd better not disturb the rest of the kitchen staff," I said swiftly as Chef Heston's face turned an unhealthy puce.

"Take your food outside, so you don't get under the feet of people who are actually working," he muttered.

"Yes, Chef," I said. He caught hold of my arm as I hurried to the chiller cabinet for the cream. "Don't think your friendship with the Princess means you can shirk your responsibilities. I'm counting every minute you're not clocked in."

I had no doubt he would be. "I promise, I'll get everything done." I raced away, made the tea, then grabbed the scones, cream, and strawberry preserves. I bustled Alice out of the kitchen and over to a bench that overlooked the gardens.

We settled with plates on our laps as we set to work on the delicious scones.

I let out a sigh of relief. Everything was back to normal. Pete's killer had been found, and I had a plate of delicious treats in front of me. It was a simple thing, but it made me smile.

Alice slathered her scone in cream, covered it in preserves, sandwiched the top and bottom together, and took a big bite. "Yum! Solving crime works up an appetite."

"At least it's solved. Dennis hated Pete. Maybe Pete taunted him about his money troubles one too many times."

"So he got rid of his competition," Alice said.

"I hope the security guards check his alibi." My gaze went to the castle. I really wanted to be in on the questioning.

"He'll only lie to them about where he was," Alice said.

"So long as he can be placed at the scene of the crime, it's only a matter of time before Dennis is charged." I bit into the sweet, light scone. "Saracen and the police will soon have everything they need."

"All thanks to us." Alice bumped her half-eaten scone against mine. "And now that's over, you have something important to focus on. You have a winning cake to make."

My insides fluttered, and I swallowed the last of my scone. "Maybe I shouldn't take part. I've had no time to prepare. The cake needs to be ready for tomorrow."

"Which gives you the whole afternoon and tonight if you need it. Your cooking never goes wrong. You have to enter. You'll let down the whole castle if you don't take part."

"I'm not representing Audley Castle. I'm only representing me."

"You're a part of the castle. It feels like you've always been here." Alice leaned against me. "I can't remember what life was like before we had your delicious cakes to enjoy. Well, I can a little. I weighed ten pounds less and was always bored. I might be a bit fatter, but I'm a hundred times happier."

Warmth flooded my chest. Alice could be ditzy, but I wouldn't have her any other way. "I feel the same."

"How about that roulade you made when we had the dull Ainsworth family over for dinner? Everyone raved about it. It even made their sullen teenage son smile and ask for seconds. It was the only time I heard him speak."

My fresh raspberry and double cream roulade had gone down well, but it didn't feel special enough for my entry. It would also be difficult to eat without making a mess. "Maybe not that."

"You did that caramel marble cake with a frosted topping, the one you made for Rupert's birthday," Alice said. "That was so beautiful. When you cut into it, all the different colors inside were divine."

"That's an idea. But I had to make six different marble cakes to get the inside just how I wanted it. I don't have the time to do that."

"I've got it! You should do a fairy theme."

I wrinkled my nose. "Are you thinking fairy cakes?"

A red scarf floated from an east turret window. It drifted down the wall and landed on top of a bush.

"Did that come from Granny's window?" Alice asked.

I peered up at her windows. A tiny figure waved madly at us. "She must want something."

Alice shook her head as she pulled out her phone. "I'm always telling her to call or text when she needs something. Granny doesn't trust phones. She thinks there's always people listening in."

She had a point. I was convinced Campbell had listening devices all around the castle. He'd probably crept into Lady Philippa's turret and made sure he could hear her conversations by planting a few bugs.

"I'll see what she needs." Alice pressed a button on her phone. "Granny, is that you throwing things at us?" She put the phone on speaker and placed it on the table.

"Am I safe now, Lady Philippa?" I asked.

"Holly, you're definitely not safe," Lady Philippa said. "Can you both hear me?"

"Of course we can," Alice said. "What do you mean? We've solved the murder. We found out who killed Pete. Holly can't be at risk."

"She absolutely is. I expect her to be dead within the next twenty-four hours. Now, be a dear and bring me up a plate of those lovely looking scones. And don't be stingy with the cream."

I gulped as I stared at the turret. "I'm still going to die?"

"We all have to die sometime," Lady Philippa said cheerfully. "At least now you can be prepared. It's important to get your affairs in order."

"We have got the right person, though?" I asked. "Dennis is the killer."

"That's for the police to figure out," Lady Philippa said. "I really am quite hungry. I might faint. I don't think I've had food sent to me for days. My cruel daughter is always forgetting about me. One day, she'll seal up this room and leave me to starve."

"You're being silly," Alice said. "We'll get you some scones." She shut off the phone and stared at me before tutting. "Don't listen to her. She's probably only saying it to get attention. You can't be at risk anymore. Dennis is locked in the saloon. Kace and Mason won't let him out."

I bit my bottom lip as I nodded. We couldn't have gotten it wrong. Dennis had the perfect motive for killing Pete. I was certain that once he'd answered all their questions, there'd be nothing to worry about.

Until then, I'd better watch my back, just in case Lady Philippa was onto something.

My arm muscles ached as I held the final pose in my plyometric session. The sun was just nosing over the trees as I shook out my arms and legs before heading back to take a shower.

I had no choice but to make an early start this morning. Not that I'd slept much the previous night. The few hours

I'd managed to grab had been full of images of elaborate cakes, and my final competition creation turning out burned and sunken in the middle. Entering baking competitions was a stressful business.

"Let's go, Meatball. Time for your food."

"Woof woof." He jumped to his feet.

I rounded the corner and walked straight into Rupert, who stood with his head down reading a book.

"Holly! Lovely to see you." He smiled at me. "You're up early today."

"It's the finals of the baking competition," I said. "I've still got lots to do before I'm ready and wanted to have a quick stretch before I got started. Get my baking muscles ready to go."

"Of course." He glanced around before reaching inside his jacket pocket. "I was hoping to see you. I got you this." He pulled out an envelope and handed it to me.

I opened it. "An annual membership to the Giddy Goat Sanctuary? What's this all about?"

He chuckled and rubbed the back of his neck. "Oh, it's nothing. I just happened to read about it online. I remembered you liked goats."

"Sure, I like goats. I like all animals."

"And you took part in that goat yoga," he said. "I had a go, but I don't have the coordination for yoga. The goats were sweet, though. And I was thinking, well, perhaps when you have a free day, we could go to the goat sanctuary together and indulge in your passion."

"Wow! That sounds fun. Would this be a friend date or a ...?" How could I ask if Rupert had romantic feelings for me without making this super awkward?

"Oh! I mean, it can be whatever you want. And there's no expectation that you have to say yes. I mean, I like goats, you like goats, so why can't we simply like goats together? Of course, if you want it to be more, that could be arranged. I don't want to force you into anything. I mean, I'd like to—"

"That's really kind of you." I placed a hand on his arm, taking pity on him as he struggled to form a complete sentence. "And yes, I'd love to see some goats with you."

He let out a huge sigh and grinned. "That's the best news I've heard all week. The sanctuary is only an hour away. We could make a day of it."

"I'd like that."

"I'll get it organized." He rubbed his hands together, turned away, and then turned back and stared at me, seeming reluctant to leave.

"Would you like to see the cake I'm entering into the competition? I've been working on it most of the night," I said.

He nodded. "A preview? Of course."

"Give me ten minutes," I said. "I need to take a shower."

"Excellent. May I help you?"

My eyebrows shot up. "You want to help me take a shower?"

"Oh! I'm such an idiot. I didn't mean that. I don't want to take a shower with you. I mean, unless, well, would you like that? No! Of course not. That's inappropriate. Oh, dear. I've forgotten what I meant to say."

I blew out a breath, feeling exhausted from watching Rupert struggle. "I can manage just fine on my own. I'll meet you in the kitchen."

"Yes! Quality idea. I look forward to it."

I dashed away, trying not to think about what had just happened. It was weird. Exciting, but weird. I stopped at the door to my apartment. A small toy goat stood at the entrance.

Meatball raced at the goat and grabbed it in his mouth.

I gently extracted it and groaned as I picked it up. It looked like I'd be getting goat gifts now Rupert thought I loved them. And I did, but they weren't my passion.

I had a super-fast shower, rough dried my hair, threw on my work uniform, and jogged back to the kitchen, with a quick detour to set Meatball up in his kennel.

Rupert was waiting with a mug in his hand. He smiled as I entered and handed me a full mug of tea.

"Thanks." I took a sip, eyeing him over the top of my mug as I did so. "And thanks for the toy goat. It's cute. Meatball also loves it. I might have a fight on my hands to keep it in one piece."

He glanced away, his cheeks glowing. "It came with the subscription to the goat sanctuary. I thought you might enjoy it. You could give him a name."

"A name! I hadn't thought about that."

"Maybe Rupert junior."

I snorted a laugh, which I quickly stifled as hurt flashed across Rupert's face. He was being serious. "Um, I'll give it some thought."

An awkward silence drifted around us, the only sounds coming from the early morning staff setting up the café for the day.

"So, where's the cake? I can't wait to see it," Rupert said.

I set my mug down. "Close your eyes. I'll get it out of the chiller cabinet." My heart thudded with excitement as I hurried over and opened the door. I pulled out my three-layered chocolate and peanut butter drip cake and placed it carefully on the counter.

I turned it a few times until I got the angle just right. "Okay, you can take a look."

He blinked and stared at the cake in silence.

My stomach flipped when he didn't say anything. "You don't like it?"

"I'm speechless. Holly, this is incredible. I think I'm in love." His gaze flashed to me before dipping back to the cake.

I grinned. "I hope it'll do. I need to add the gold roses as decoration, but it's almost done."

"I'm sure you'll win. You've already won my heart with it."

"I'll make sure to save you a slice once the judging is over." I grabbed my mug and took a slurp.

"I look forward to trying it," he said.

The kitchen door banged open, and Saracen walked in.

"Hey! Should you be here?" I asked.

He nodded. "The doc's okayed me to come back to work. We need to talk."

Chapter 16

After carefully placing the cake back in the chiller cabinet, I hurried out of the kitchen after Saracen. "Is something wrong?"

He raised a hand and pulled his phone from his suit jacket pocket. "We're both here, Campbell."

My eyebrows shot up. "I thought Campbell was busy saving the world and shouldn't be contacted?"

"I can be contacted. I just prefer to be the one who does the contacting," Campbell said on the other end of the phone. "Holly, you've not been following my orders."

"Um, remind me what my orders were again?" What had I done wrong? We'd caught the killer.

"To update Saracen as to your movements and progress with questioning suspects in Pete Saunder's murder. Note the heavy emphasis on questioning only."

"I have been doing just that! I've been checking in with Saracen all the time. We even had breakfast together the other morning. We talked about the case."

"You're making him breakfast? Why don't I ever get breakfast from you?" Campbell asked.

"Because Saracen's a lot nicer to me than you are," I said.

Saracen grinned. "The police and our security have been working together. Dennis is still protesting his innocence, though."

"What about his alibi?" I asked.

Campbell muttered something I couldn't hear. I doubted it was complimentary. "Yes, tell us about that, Saracen."

"Dennis claimed he was on his food truck at the time of the murder. He packed up early because sales were slow."

"Any witnesses?" Campbell asked.

"None that can confirm he was there at the time of the murder. However, there's a problem."

"What's that?" I asked at the same time as Campbell.

"There are no fingerprints on the laptop that are a match to Dennis."

"He must have taken it," I said. "Otherwise, what was it doing in his truck? Maybe he wore gloves when he used it. I used some food prep gloves when we were looking at the laptop, so I wouldn't leave fingerprints. He could have done the same."

"I didn't know you'd been snooping around on Pete's laptop," Campbell said. "Was that something I instructed you to do?"

I winced. "It was only for a few minutes. I didn't do any damage."

"Is there any DNA on the laptop that might implicate Dennis?" Campbell asked.

"Nothing," Saracen said. "No hairs, no skin fibers. If he took the laptop, he didn't use it."

"You know, I've been thinking." I tapped my fingers together.

"This sounds dangerous," Campbell said.

I glared at the phone. "Dennis was shocked when I sat on the laptop."

"You *sat* on the stolen laptop?" Campbell said.

"By accident. Dennis was getting a bit full on when we were found in his food truck. I stumbled backward to get out of his way. The laptop was under the cushion I landed on. Which is a terrible hiding place. Anyone who did a search of the truck would have found it. What if …" I wasn't sure whether to voice my concerns. "What if somebody put the laptop in the food truck?"

"I thought everyone was convinced that Dennis killed Pete?" Campbell said.

"I'm not disagreeing with that," I said. "He has been going around telling people he's glad Pete was killed. But the lack of evidence on the laptop and his shock when it was found got me wondering. How much have you looked into Ricky Stormy's background?"

"You still think he could be a suspect?" Saracen asked.

"He has a pretty good alibi, but he may have snuck out of the pub and gone to the food fair. If he used a car, it would only take fifteen minutes to get there and back. Elspeth might not have noticed he was gone. Then there's the issue with the money. We looked at Pete's bank account. He was making monthly payments to Ricky. I wondered if Ricky had loaned him more money and that's what he was having trouble getting back from Pete."

"Saracen, have you been in the loop on this the whole time?" Campbell asked. "Holly's telling me things I've not heard before."

"Don't blame Saracen for not passing things on. I may have forgotten to tell him a few tiny things. And you can hardly blame him if he's struggling. You whizzed nearly the whole security team away from the castle on your top secret mission. Saracen's doing an amazing job."

Saracen's eyes widened, and he cleared his throat. "Everything's good here, boss. I'm not struggling with anything."

"It is. And I've been looking after things when Saracen's not been well. I mean, when he's not been around. You know, busy keeping everyone safe." Oops! I shrugged an apology at Saracen. I'd just put my foot in it.

"What's this? What's going on over there?" Campbell's tone was suspicious. "You're sick, Saracen?"

"Nope. Good as new, boss. Everything's under control. Dennis is still the prime suspect. That's our focus."

"Good job. Keep an eye on Ricky, though. Just make sure the police keep their attention on Dennis. He's a solid suspect. He was found with the victim's laptop in his possession, and he has a lousy alibi."

"Just playing devil's advocate for a second, but why did he take the laptop?" I asked. "We couldn't find anything on there."

"Leave that to my tech team," Campbell said. "You might have missed something."

"That's very possible. After all, I don't have a team of cyber tech experts on standby, ready to drop everything and help me save the world."

"Very true. Saracen, tie up any loose ends and let's finish this."

"But what about—"

"That's an end to it." Campbell cut me off. "Dennis will be charged. Get back to the kitchen, Holly. You do your best work there."

My jaw dropped. Had he really just said that?

Saracen winced. "I'm on it, boss." He ended the call and turned to me. "Campbell can be abrupt when he's mission focused. Try not to hold it against him."

"Don't worry, I know my place, tied to the kitchen table just like Campbell wants." I flushed. "I didn't mean it like that. I see now that Campbell only makes use of me when it suits his schedule. This is the last time I'll help him."

"Holly, cut the guy some slack. He's stressed. He's dealing with an ... No, I can't tell you."

"Go on! If I know what he's dealing with, I might be more understanding." I longed to know what secret mission Campbell and his team were on. "It has to be something huge. Has a member of the royal family done something they shouldn't?"

"I can't say. But the mission is going well. And you put in the leg work on this and solved the murder. Campbell won't forget that."

"He's already forgotten," I said. "I still think we should look more closely at Ricky. We need to cover all the bases."

"They've been covered. You did great work." He ducked his head. "And thanks for not revealing what's wrong—"

I slapped a hand over Saracen's mouth and shook my head.

He removed my hand and glared at me. "What are you doing?"

I circled my finger in the air. "You never know who could be listening."

Saracen looked along the empty corridor. "No one's listening into our conversation."

"It's probably best not to talk about ... personal matters."

Saracen's head jerked back as he roared with laughter. "No way! You think Campbell's got the castle bugged?"

"Shush! He'll hear you. He has bugs everywhere."

He clutched his middle and bent over, the laughter continuing. "Holly, you're hilarious. Of course he hasn't done that. That's illegal. This is a private family home. I can guarantee, Campbell doesn't bug the castle."

"How come he knows things he shouldn't? Unless he's listening at keyholes when I'm having conversations, he must bug the place. That's the only explanation."

Saracen continued to chuckle. "Campbell's crazy over the top observant. And he's like a silent, deadly panther. If he doesn't want you to know he's around, then you won't. That's how he gets the inside information in the castle. It's got nothing to do with bugs hidden in the light sockets."

I sighed. It was a stretch of the imagination to imagine Campbell skulking around and hiding bugs everywhere. "Maybe you're right."

"I am. This case is as good as closed. And you do need to get back to your cakes. I know you're representing Audley Castle today."

"Not in an official capacity," I said. "I have made something, though. Hopefully it'll be good enough to get a place."

"Hey, I've never heard you so full of doubt before. Your cakes are amazing. They were worth me upsetting my diabetes."

I stared at him and pointed around the ceiling. "Remember, someone is always listening in."

"Campbell isn't listening to this conversation."

"Well, if he suddenly mentions your health condition, you'll know how he found out about it. These walls have ears."

"No, these walls are just solid, so you don't hear when someone's walking past the door when you're having a private conversation. That's all it is."

I was still going to be careful about what I said. "I should get back to the kitchen. I left Lord Rupert on his own. He must think something strange is going on."

"Good luck with your baking competition today," Saracen said.

"Thanks." I turned and headed back into the kitchen. I was worrying about nothing. I hadn't mentioned Lady Philippa's warning about my safety; it would only make

Campbell laugh at me. But that was the reason I was having some doubt about Dennis's guilt.

Rupert walked through the external kitchen door as I entered. "I've being doing some undercover sleuthing on your behalf."

"You have? Who have you been spying on?"

"The other finalists in the competition. Some of them are in the marquee."

My stomach flipped over. "Already? But I haven't finished. Is the food out?"

"I spotted a few things. Some of them have large cool boxes next to their tables. It's not long to go now until they start laying out. Do you want to take a look?"

"I absolutely do. Lead the way." I walked to the marquee and found all the finalists were setting up.

There were three different categories that would be judged: savory food, the dessert category, which I'd be in, and beverages. There were ten finalists in each category, and each entry would be judged by four judges. The Duke and Duchess, and two food and drink experts who'd been brought in for the contest. All the taste tests would be done blind, so the judges would have no idea whose entry they were sampling.

Nerves fluttered inside me as I looked around.

"Where do you want to start?" Rupert asked.

"Let's begin in the drinks category." I walked past tables representing sparkling wines, locally produced white wine, and a variety of spirits. Everyone looked very serious and professional.

"There's less than hour to go until judging," Rupert said. "How are you feeling?"

I groaned. "Sick now you've told me how little time I have."

He patted my arm. "You'll be amazing. How about we take a look around the savouries, see who your competition is there?"

Although most of the food wasn't laid out, Colin's cheese table was there, as was Maisie's pie stand, only missing the pie. It looked like she'd been up early decorating the stand. There were several other savory pie entrants, a dried pork entry, and a seed company, promoting roasted, flavored produce.

"My mouth's watering," Rupert said. "It's a shame I'm not a judge."

"It is. Then I'd be able to bribe you into letting me win."

"You wouldn't need to bribe me," he said. "You're bound to win."

I was buoyed by his enthusiastic support. "Okay, I'm ready. Let's take a look at the desserts."

There were two speciality chocolate stands, a sweet pie seller, three cake stands, my own stand, and the remaining finalists looked like they'd be serving cookies or pastries as their entry.

The displays looked professional with banners, printed signs, and decorations. I hadn't given any thought into what I'd put on my stand. I was hoping the cake would speak for itself. Now, I felt a bit amateurish.

"I've seen enough," I said. "I need to get back and make the finishing touches to the cake before the kitchen gets busy."

"I should get back too," Rupert said. "I'll catch up with you after the judging. Best of luck." He gave my arm a reassuring squeeze before hurrying off toward the castle.

I took one last look around the marquee before heading to the exit. I could do this. I was good enough. I'd spent years perfecting my recipes. My entry could stand against all of these. I felt quietly confident as I left the marquee.

I tilted my head at the sound of a male voice I recognized. Rather than heading to the castle kitchen, I walked around the side of the marquee.

Ricky Stormy stood with his back to me on the phone. "I've already said, everything's in hand. I had an unexpected opening, so you're in if you want to be a part of the deal."

I stayed where I was and continued to listen.

"You know how this works. I need the money upfront before you get the delivery." He was silent for a few seconds. "That's the arrangement I have with everyone."

Whatever deal he was making, it didn't sound legitimate if it needed to be upfront cash in hand.

"Everyone else is happy. You get the product and the repackaging tools. All you have to do is stump up for the labor to get the cheap pies in the fancy boxes. Then you sell them as premium products. Customers are suckers. They see an expensive label and a fancy box and they'll pay double what it's worth. Sometimes triple."

Ricky was getting cheap pies and duping people into thinking they were buying top quality? Had he had that deal with Pete? That must have been why Pete could sell his products so cheaply.

Ricky strode along the side of the marquee.

I crept along behind him, determined to hear everything.

"I've got other people who want this deal. An old business partner has decided to … retire unexpectedly. It happened a couple of days ago. Are you in or not?"

He must be talking about Pete.

"You don't need to know where the pies come from. That's my problem. You repackage and sell them to whoever you like. I don't give you the supply leads, but I guarantee you'll make a profit. Give me the money, and I'll do the rest."

I frowned. Ricky was a thief and a cheat.

"No, you can't speak to the others. They know a great deal when they see one. You need to keep this on the down low. No talking about where your pies come from. If any questions get asked, you plead ignorance. Stick with me, and I'll make you rich."

This was a motive for murder. What if Pete had decided to blackmail Ricky about his dodgy business methods? Ricky could have murdered Pete to ensure his corrupt business model wasn't leaked to the authorities.

Ricky was dodgy, and he'd been in a dispute with Pete just before he'd died. It had to be connected.

Ricky spun around and stared at me. "I'll call you back. Take a little time to think about it."

I backed up, my heart thudding. There was nowhere to hide, and it was obvious I'd been listening. How was I going to talk my way out of this one?

Chapter 17

"It's Holly, isn't it?" Ricky strode over as he shoved his phone into his pocket. "What are you doing around the back of this marquee?"

I swallowed my nerves. "I'm a finalist in the food fair competition."

His narrowed gaze ran over me. "How much of that conversation did you hear?"

I lifted my chin. "Enough to know that it gives you a motive for killing Pete."

"Killing Pete!" He grinned. "I thought we'd been over that already. Why would I do that? He was a good client. Paid on time mostly and shifted all the stock I supplied. It worked for both of us. My business is legitimate and successful."

"You call stealing pies and selling them on as premium products legitimate?"

His grin faded and was replaced by a scowl. "You heard everything. That's unfortunate. Who are you going to tell this bit of news?"

"I bet you haven't told the police about your business."

"They won't be interested. They're focused on serious crime, not some minor discrepancies in product description."

It was a lot more than that. "Is this the reason you killed Pete?"

He scraped a hand through his hair. "You'll give me a complex. Stop saying that. I didn't kill the guy."

"You had reasons for wanting him dead. But it wasn't about the loan. He was paying you back. What else did he do to anger you?"

"How exactly do you know about my finances?"

I gulped. "I have … friends in high places. These friends looked at Pete's bank account and saw a monthly payment going to you. If you weren't arguing about that on the day of the food fair, what was your argument about?"

"Who said we argued? And you already know my alibi. You got your goon to beat it out of me when I was outside the pub. I bet you checked it too, so you know I'm being honest with you."

"Your alibi may have been checked," I said. "But you're still guilty."

"Not of murder, though. I may have a shady past, but I don't want murder on my record. Where's this crazy theory coming from? The last thing I heard, the police had someone locked up for Pete's murder."

"There is someone they're talking to, but it's not a closed case. What was your disagreement with Pete about?"

Ricky cocked his head. "Nosy one, aren't you?"

"Curious."

"I have several sidelines to my business. Moneylending is one of them. People come to me when they have an emergency situation and need money fast. Maybe that's what happened with Pete. And sometimes, when a person has an emergency, they're not thinking straight. I needed to give Pete a friendly nudge, so he didn't forget his obligations."

"You're a loan shark?"

"That's a term I despise. It sounds so ruthless. I'm here when people have a need that can't be met by the usual borrowing organizations."

"This emergency loan you gave Pete was what you talked about? He stopped paying you back, and you decided to teach him a lesson?"

"It didn't happen. Pete knows my reputation. That's more than enough to keep him on the straight and narrow. He just forgot his priorities. I thought he might make a run for it and forget what he owed me. After our chat, he was happy to sort out a schedule of repayments. It's just a shame some idiot stabbed him before I got my money back."

That was a valid point. Now Pete was dead, Ricky wouldn't be able to get his money back easily. "Did Pete know where his pies came from?" I asked.

"Of course he did. He didn't care. I wondered whether that cute assistant of his might be interested in using the same supply chain. I tried to talk to her about it, but she shut me down. I'm hoping to change her mind if my other lead comes to nothing."

"Maisie wouldn't be interested in anything so corrupt," I said.

"Yeah, you clearly don't know her. She's ambitious. Didn't you notice how quick she was to fill Pete's shoes? I bet she takes his food truck as well. I've got my eye on that. That'll cover the loan repayments if I sell it. She might be young, but she's not stupid. If you've got any doubts about the police having the right person, maybe you should look at Little Miss I'm-Not-So-Innocent. She's landed on her feet now Pete's dead. And I hear she's a finalist in this competition. You see, she's already going places thanks to Pete being dead."

I'd discounted Maisie as a suspect, but I was now having doubts about everyone. I'd missed a piece of the puzzle along the way. I didn't think Maisie had killed Pete, but Ricky was right, she had a lot to gain from his murder, and she had a small window of opportunity to kill him.

And I was having doubts about Dennis. What if that laptop I found had been planted?

If it wasn't Ricky who killed Pete, and it wasn't Dennis, then maybe it was Maisie.

"Listen, this can be our little secret." Ricky edged closer. "No one needs to know about my business. Everyone's got to earn a living somehow."

"I can't keep quiet about a crime," I said.

"It's just an entrepreneurial spirit that's gotten bent out of shape. No one's coming to any harm."

"What about the people you're stealing from?"

"Things always go missing when they're imported. People miscount boxes on trucks and write down the wrong information. No one's out of pocket. And if anyone does discover things missing, they claim them back on the insurance." He jabbed a finger at me. "Don't tell anyone about this."

I backed up as Ricky advanced toward me. "What are you going to do if I tell somebody?"

"Holly! There you are." Rupert strode toward me.

Ricky instantly backed off and stuffed his hands into his pockets.

I glared at him before hurrying toward Rupert. "I was on my way. I just got a bit distracted."

"I thought I should warn you, Alice has decided to take over."

"Take over what?"

"She's carrying your cake to the marquee."

My heart froze. Alice was known for being less than dainty, especially when she got excited. "That's very …

good of her." Or it would be until she tripped over the hem of her dress and sent the cake flying.

"She wanted to help. I said she should wait for you to come back, but she wants it to be a surprise."

"Thanks, Rupert." I shot a glare at Ricky, who was looking on unhappily. I didn't like to think about what he had planned for me if I revealed his pie scandal, but that was the least of my worries.

I had to get to the marquee before Alice dropped my beautiful cake.

Chapter 18

I shot through the entrance to the marquee and jogged to the table. Alice was just bending down, my cake in her outstretched arms. She placed it on the table and stepped back.

I blew out a huge breath of relief. The cake had made it in one piece.

She turned when she saw me and grinned. "Surprise! I wanted to do something useful. Doesn't it look beautiful?"

I studied the cake carefully. The distressed chocolate icing looked perfect. "It looks great. Thanks, Alice. There are a few finishing touches I want to add to it, but I can do that here."

My head shot up as Meatball's frantic barking reached my ears. He shouldn't be out of his kennel. I hurried to the marquee entrance and peered outside.

Meatball was racing toward the marquee with four of the Duchess's corgis on his heels. His fur was sticking up, suggesting they'd had a rough and tumble before he'd escaped. Among the pack was his new furry best friend, Priscilla. Although it looked like they weren't friends anymore.

Alice joined me by the entrance. "Is Meatball okay?"

"No! He's being bullied by those spoiled corgis again. They love chasing him."

"They look like they've been having fun," Alice said.

"They pick on him," I said. "He's the friendliest dog around and only wants to have some doggy buddies to hang out with."

"He's running awfully fast," Alice said. "And he's heading straight for the marquee."

"We'd better head the corgis off before they get inside and eat the food." I hurried out with Alice, and we stood guard at the entrance.

Meatball didn't slow as he bounded toward me. His back legs coiled, and he launched into my arms, landing with a thud against my chest.

He licked my cheek before turning and growling at the fast approaching corgis.

"Don't worry! I'll deal with this lot." Alice stood with her arms and legs flung out. "They're not getting past me."

The corgis kept coming, racing closer. They weren't slowing down.

Alice waved her arms in the air. "Shoo! Off you go now. Bad dogs."

Two of the corgis darted past Alice and into the marquee.

My eyes widened as they raced around barking at each other and anyone who got too close.

Meatball squirmed out of my arms, dropped to the ground, and raced after the corgis.

"No! Wait! Don't go in there." I hurried in after him.

The other two corgis dodged past Alice. She tried to rugby tackle one but ended up face first on the ground outside the marquee.

I ran back and helped her to her feet. "We have to get these corgis out of here."

Chaos greeted us as we entered the marquee. Several competition entrants were guarding their stands as if their lives depended on it. One corgi was already on top of a table chewing on a slab of dried meat.

I looked around and was grateful that Meatball was simply dodging under the tables and trying to avoid another fight with the rest of the corgis.

There was a scream as something smashed to the ground. A pie display had been shoved over by a corgi. Two of them were stuffing their faces with the contents of the destroyed pies.

"Stop those dogs!" someone yelled.

"They belong to the Duchess," another person shouted.

"I don't care whose dogs they are. They're a menace. They'll destroy everything if we don't stop them."

I hurried to my stand and stood guard in front of the cake. After going to all this effort, I wasn't letting the Duchess's bratty corgis ruin this for me.

"Away with you." I flapped my arms at two corgis as they headed toward me. They veered off at the last second, yipping angrily as they spotted Meatball racing around the other side of the marquee with something that looked suspiciously like a sausage sticking out of his mouth.

I groaned as the corgis smashed into another table and the contents spilled to the ground.

This was a disaster. Although I suppose it was eliminating some of my competition. At this rate, there wouldn't even be a contest. The corgis and Meatball would have destroyed everything and eaten all the food.

"I've got one!" Alice held up a squirming corgi, his mouth full of food.

"I've got one as well." Rupert stood on the other side of the marquee, a corgi tucked under his arm.

"We'll handle the rest," another stallholder yelled as he dashed toward the final two corgis and Meatball, a large red sausage raised like a bat.

I raced over and caught Meatball as he dashed past. "You're not going anywhere. We don't want your good name associated with this band of furry hooligans."

The rest of the stallholders shooed the final two corgis out.

"We'll get them all back to the castle," Alice said as she hurried out with Rupert.

The chaos the dogs had left behind was impressive. Three stands were ruined, and several displays looked like they'd been stomped on. With less than an hour to go, we had a job on our hands to fix this.

The marquee was abuzz with activity as people pulled the displays together and resurrected what was left of their food.

I turned and looked at my cake. Thank goodness they hadn't touched it. It was still perfect. Just a few finishing touches, and I'd be all set to go.

"The dogs are dealt with." Rupert strode into the marquee with Alice a few moments later.

"And I've gotten Meatball under control," I said. "This wasn't his fault. Those corgis love to tease him."

Alice petted Meatball's head. "We don't blame him for this. This lovely chap could never do anything as malicious as those corgis. Don't forget, I've grown up with those beasts. The way they behave, you'd think they owned the castle."

"I hope everyone can pull things together before the contest starts," Rupert said. He looked over at my cake. "At least your entry is untouched."

"I'm grateful for that," I said. "I just need to finish dressing it."

"We'll keep an eye on the cake if you need to get things from the kitchen," Rupert said.

"That would be great. And I need to get Meatball back in his kennel and settle him down after the excitement. I'll be ten minutes."

"Take as long as you need," Rupert said. "We can help the other stallholders and see if we can't put things back together."

I'd just reached the exit to the marquee when there was a loud thud and a crack.

Several people gasped, and I spun around.

My heart sank to the floor. Rupert lay on the ground, his arms splayed out, and his face in my cake.

I placed Meatball on the ground and raced back. "What … what happened? My cake. You … you've destroyed it."

Alice extracted Rupert from the now ruined cake. "He tripped over his own feet. He's always doing that."

Rupert wiped cake out of his eyes. "I … I don't know what happened. I turned around, and it felt like I'd tripped on something."

"You tripped over yourself," Alice said with a loud tut. "Look what you've done. Holly's cake is squished."

His shoulders slumped as he held the destroyed cake in his hands. "Holly, I don't know what to say. Your beautiful cake. My clumsiness has ruined it for you."

I blinked as fast as I could, but tears kept springing up in my eyes. I'd worked so hard on this. I wanted to win this contest, and now it had been taken from me.

I tried to speak, but couldn't get the words out.

"Wait! This isn't ruined." Alice grabbed my arm and shook me. "Holly, we can fix this."

I gestured to the mess on the ground as several stallholders came over and muttered words of astonishment and condolence. "How can we fix this?"

"Maybe not this cake, but we'll do something else." Alice nudged her brother, who was still on his knees covered in cake. "Clean up this mess. I'll help Holly figure this out."

The stallholders murmured in surprise as Alice bossed Rupert around.

He nodded. "Of course. You won't even know this happened when you get back. Well, obviously the cake won't be here." Rupert stood slowly and brushed cake off his shirt.

I swallowed, my throat tight and my jaw wobbling.

Rupert shot me a guilt-filled glance. "Please say you forgive me. If it's any consolation, from what I tasted, it was absolutely delicious."

I pinched the bridge of my nose and closed my eyes, trying as hard as possible not to scream. It was no consolation.

A not so gentle prod from Alice made me open my eyes. "Let's see what we can salvage in the kitchen."

I nodded mutely. I should say everything was fine and tell Rupert not to worry, but I was angry at him. Usually, I found his clumsiness endearing, but it had just cost me my spot in this competition.

"Let's get out of here." Alice grabbed my arm and dragged me away from the car crash of a cake that lay scattered on the ground.

My energy faded as she dragged me to the kitchen. I couldn't do this. It was too much work. "I'm withdrawing. There's no time to bake anything from scratch. Besides, the contest shouldn't even go ahead after the corgis have ruined other people's entries."

"Don't talk like that. We'll find a solution." Her fingers wrapped around mine. "We can do this. One little cake malfunction shouldn't derail you."

"That was more than a malfunction. That was the Mount Vesuvius of cake catastrophes."

The morning rush was in full swing as we entered the kitchen.

Chef Heston dashed over as soon as he saw me. "Step to it. We need more sausage rolls and some extra ..." He took a step back. "What's the matter with you? You look like you've seen a ghost."

"Rupert killed her cake," Alice said. "We need something to take its place."

"Take its place? You can't take cake from the kitchen," Chef Heston said. "That wouldn't be fair on everyone else."

"You're right." Despair wrapped around me like a stale blanket. "And it's too late to make anything else. I'm withdrawing."

"Hold on a moment," Chef Heston said. "You make fifty percent of the desserts in this kitchen. Technically, the things you make are yours."

I scrubbed a hand across my face. "Are you serious? You'd let me use anything in here that I've already made?"

"I'm not sure what you can do with muffins, scones, and chocolate sponge, but why not?" Chef Heston nodded. "Do your best, Holly. Don't worry about the sausage rolls; I'll deal with them."

I was too stunned to speak. I must have caught Chef Heston on a good day.

Alice hugged me as he walked away. "You see! We can do something. You've got lots of choice here."

I pulled back from her hug and walked to the chiller cabinet, still full of uncertainty. There was a pineapple upside down cake, a bread pudding, four types of muffins, cherry scones, fairy cakes, apple turnovers, and two Bakewell tarts.

Alice wrapped an arm around my shoulders. "How about a croquembouche? I love a mountain of cream and chocolate. That would be sure to tempt the judges."

"There's no time to make that," I said. "We don't serve it in the café, it's too fiddly. I wouldn't have time to make the choux pastry and let it cool before adding the fillings and the toppings. If you try to fill them warm, the cream goes rancid, and the chocolate slides off."

"Hmmm. What about a different take on a croquembouche? Use those muffins. You could hollow out the center, fill them with whatever you like, and stack them up."

I peered at the muffins. We had gone overboard on baking chocolate and raspberry muffins. These wouldn't all get eaten today, and they didn't stay fresh for long. "I guess I could stack them and use icing as a glue."

"Yes! And put decorations on. Those muffins will look so pretty." Alice clapped her hands. "So, you'll give it a go?"

I stared at the muffins. Would that work? I opened the chiller cabinet and pulled out a plate of muffins. I tried a couple of different ways to stack them. "I'll need thick icing to get these to stick together. Given their shape, they won't form a stack as easily as choux pastry."

"You think it could work?" Alice grabbed a muffin and took a bite.

Hope lit a fire in my chest. "It's got possibilities."

Chef Heston strode over. "So, are you withdrawing from the competition?"

"Not so long as you let me have all the chocolate and raspberry muffins you've got in the café. Princess Alice has given me a great idea. It might just work."

He pursed his lips and stared at the muffins. "They're all yours. I'll bring through any we've got out for sale if that'll help."

I grinned, kissed his cheek, and nodded. "Yes. That will be perfect."

He scowled at me, but there was the hint of a smile on his face. "Don't get carried away. And don't think I'm not marking the amount of time this is taking you from your job."

I chuckled. "Thanks, Chef."

He grumbled again before hurrying to the main café and returning with a tray of muffins.

"What do you need me to do?" Alice asked.

"Keep your brother out of the way so he doesn't face plant in this." I pulled out different colored icing, a piping bag, cream, a variety of different decorations to put on the top, and laid out the muffins in front of me.

Alice was silent for a moment as she watched me work. "Don't be too hard on him. Rupert's so clumsy. It runs in the family. He was excited to help you. I could tell he was mortified."

"I know it wasn't deliberate. I just wish he hadn't landed on top of my cake."

"He did say it tasted nice," Alice said. "Some of it splattered on me as well, and I agree about how tasty it was. The cake was perfect."

I puffed out a breath. "I'm not creating perfection this time. Let's see what we can do with these muffins, though."

The next forty minutes had me focused on hollowing out muffins, mixing different batches of icing, borrowing as much cream as I could from the kitchen fridge, and finding a way to stack a tower of muffins without them toppling.

The whole time I worked, Alice sat silently and patiently by the counter. I'd never seen her so still. Admittedly, she ate three muffins while I worked, but she didn't say a word.

I squeezed a globule of chocolate icing on the base of the last muffin and placed it carefully on the top of the stack. It was eight layers high, each muffin glued to the next with chocolate icing. The muffins were filled with either a rich caramel sauce, a dark chocolate sauce, or thick cream.

"That looks yummy," Alice said quietly.

"I'm not done yet." I smiled at her. "I'm going to drizzle dark chocolate and caramel sauce all over the muffins and top with edible flowers."

"That sounds even yummier." Alice squeezed my arm as I walked past her toward the kitchen door. "I knew you'd do it."

I stopped as I reached the door and looked back at her. "We did it. If it wasn't for you, I'd have thrown in my apron and admitted defeat. I'd never have thought about making a croquembouche out of muffins."

She grinned, chocolate muffin stuck between her teeth. "I'm a genius in the making. Happy to help."

After a quick hunt around the flower garden, I found just what I needed. Some delicate primula gold lace petals. The burst of red would accent the rich dark of the chocolate muffins and bring out a hint of the cherries studded throughout the stack.

I hurried back to the kitchen and spent a minute washing the flowers and then icing them carefully to the muffins. Just a few. I wanted this to look extravagantly tasteful.

"Shall I carry it out?" Alice asked.

My eyes narrowed. "Best I take charge of this. You be on Rupert watch. If he gets within ten feet of this dessert, he'll be in trouble."

We hurried to the marquee with less than five minutes to spare before the contest closed to entrants.

Rupert had been true to his word, and a pristine white cloth covered my empty table. My eyes widened at the incredible display of flowers placed on the table. The colors fit perfectly with the primula decorations on my muffins. It was as if Rupert knew exactly what I'd been planning.

My eyes teared up again, but I didn't have time to think about it. With only a few minutes left, I placed my tower of muffins down and blew out a breath.

Alice hugged me. "Now all we can do is wait to see how amazing the judges think this is. Then we celebrate."

I leaned into her hug. All I wanted to do was put my feet up and eat one of those muffins glistening alluringly at me. But Alice was right, my part in this was over.

Two tense hours had passed since I last saw my competition entry. All the finalists in the contest had to leave the marquee so the judging was fair and impartial.

I tried to focus on my work in the kitchen, but all I could think about was what the judges thought of my last minute entry. Did it stand up against the others? What if the chocolate icing had melted and all the muffins sat in a gloopy heap on the table?

The kitchen door opened, and Alice bounced through. "They're about to make the announcement. Come on! You don't want to miss this."

Nerves rattled through me as Alice caught hold of my hand and tugged me along. "I ... I'm not ready."

"You are! You've got nothing to worry about. I snuck a look into the marquee and they've eaten a lot of your muffins. Much more than anyone else's dessert. You're sure to win."

I wasn't so sure about that, but I'd remain as positive as I could. After all, who didn't love a stack of gooey muffins covered in chocolate drizzle?

As we neared the marquee, Rupert appeared, holding a huge bouquet of red roses. He thrust them toward me.

"Please forgive me, Holly. These are for you."

I stared at the roses. "You didn't have to do that."

"Holly doesn't have time for your gifts," Alice said. "The judges are about to announce their decision. We need to find out what Holly's won."

I took the roses from Rupert. "They're beautiful. Thank you."

He nodded before following along behind us.

I no longer felt angry with him. If anything, I was feeling guilty. I'd been so stunned when he'd fallen on my cake that I'd let my anger get the better of me. Everyone made mistakes. Rupert hadn't meant it maliciously, and I'd reacted badly.

There was a small crowd in the marquee as we entered. Alice strode straight to the front, pulling me with her.

"We must get a good spot," she whispered. "That'll make it easy for you to go up and get your prize."

"Don't be so sure I'm winning anything," I muttered. "There's lots of incredible food here."

She squeezed my hand tightly and turned to face the judges who stood in front of us, waiting to give the announcement.

"Welcome, everybody." A smartly dressed middle-aged woman with a neat dark bob and a warm smile looked around. "I'm Eliza Mackintosh, head judge. I must say, we've had a marvelous afternoon tasting the delicious food and sampling the drink. We've had some of the county's best wine, delicious savory treats, and so many desserts that I'm fairly certain I'll need to book an emergency dental appointment. It was all so wonderful."

A nervous chuckle ran through the waiting crowd.

"Those of you who have received a special commendation, and there is one for each category, will find a card on your table. You'll each receive a prize along with your commendation."

Several heads turned as people looked at their tables to see if they had a card. I forced myself not to, but it was tempting to take a peek.

"But of course," Eliza said, "you're most interested in who has won the grand prize and is the overall winner." She turned to the Duchess.

She nodded and stepped forward, smiling at the crowd as she looked around. "Before I announce the three winners, I'd like to say that the produce today was excellent. I have your details and will be placing plenty of orders from you in the future. Your food and drink will grace our tables for many years to come."

Several people nodded and smiled, happy to be serving the castle. It was a big feather in their caps.

"On to the winners." She lifted a small card and held it in front of her. "In third place, the award goes to the Fine Cheese Company. We all agreed it was a marvelously rich and tangy product."

Everyone clapped, and a man stepped forward and accepted an envelope and a small trophy from the Duchess.

She looked around. "Second prize goes to ... Holly Holmes, for her delicious and inventive muffin dessert."

"Second place," Alice whispered as she pushed me forward and took my roses from me so that my hands were free. "Well done."

I mustered a smile. That was great. Really good. I was happy. Although it would have been brilliant to win.

The Duchess leaned forward and pressed a kiss on my cheek as I accepted my prize. "Excellent dessert, Holly. I didn't like to say to the other judges, but I recognized your trademark work. Absolutely scrumptious, and such a clever use of muffins. It must have taken you a long time to come up with that concept."

I stepped back and smiled. "You'd be surprised. And I had a little help to come up with the idea."

She nodded as I stepped back to Alice's side, my trophy clutched in my hand.

Rupert appeared on my other side and leaned down. "I'm so sorry you didn't win. This is all my fault. If there's anything—"

"You don't need to keep saying sorry." I touched his arm and gave him my warmest smile. "It was an accident."

"I hate myself. All that hard work destroyed by my clumsiness."

"No, don't think like that. I was angry with you and that was wrong. You were only trying to be helpful. And I got second prize. Plus, we get to eat a mountain of muffins after this is finished."

He shrugged and smiled. "Anything I can do to make up for it, just say."

"We're already going to see some goats together."

"Oh! You still want to do that, after—"

"Stop! And yes, I do." My friendship with Rupert was strong. I'd get over my squashed cake.

A tap on my shoulder had me turning. Saracen stood behind me, a stern expression on his face.

"Is something wrong?" I stepped away just as a speciality chocolate company was announced as first prize winner.

Saracen led me away from the small crowd. "I've got bad news. Dennis has been released. He's not Pete's killer."

Chapter 19

I stumbled out of the marquee, still not believing what I'd just heard. "You're sure Dennis Lambeth is innocent?" I asked Saracen.

"What's going on?" Alice raced out behind us.

I sucked in a deep breath. "We need muffins, and now."

"I'll grab your cake from the table." Alice flung my roses back at me. "Don't gossip while I'm away."

I turned back to Saracen. "No cake for you."

He raised a hand. "I've learned my lesson. I'll stay away from it, although I was drooling when I looked at it earlier. It's like a delicious torture. It's so bad for me, but it looks so good."

Alice emerged from the marquee, the tray with my muffin stack firmly in her hands. Rupert was beside her.

"Let's take this somewhere quiet." I led the group to a bench beside the castle rose garden and we all sat.

Alice got to work on deconstructing my muffin stack before handing them around. "So, what's going on?"

Saracen stared longingly at the muffins before dragging his gaze to me. "A witness has come forward. Dennis was seen on his food truck at the time of the murder. His alibi checks out. He couldn't have killed Pete."

Alice took a large bite of muffin. "Then who did?"

Rupert glanced at me. "You were talking to that chap earlier today outside the marquee. It seemed intense. Do you think he had something to do with it?"

I glanced at Saracen. "Ricky Stormy. I overheard an interesting conversation with a potential business partner. Ricky's been selling stolen pies. He changes the product packaging and passes it to distributors who sell it on as a premium product. I'm not sure of the details, but it sounds like he's stealing pies when they're imported into the country."

"It's not him. Ricky has an alibi," Saracen said.

I nodded. "He was chatting up Elspeth. She confirmed it. Although there's a small window of opportunity. Ricky could have snuck out of the pub, but it doesn't seem likely. He had a good motive for wanting Pete out of the way, but he also wanted his money back. With Pete dead, that presents Ricky with a problem."

"We've discounted the others," Saracen said. "The ex-girlfriend, Jessica, was at the food fair buying up last-minute bargains."

"Again, there's a small window of opportunity for her to have killed Pete," I said.

"She could have snuck up on him and killed him," Alice said.

"And then carried on with her shopping as if nothing happened?" Saracen asked.

"Some women find shopping very relaxing. Maybe she stabbed and then shopped to calm her nerves," Alice said.

I shook my head. "Jessica was open about the problems she'd had with Pete. Their relationship had failed, and she'd moved on. She wasn't holding a grudge. I don't think we need to look at her again."

"Then we have Maisie and Colin," Saracen said.

"They were at the food fair but were busy packing up their stands and putting things away. They were seen by lots of people." I tapped my fingers on the bench. "I wondered about Maisie, though. Her luck has definitely changed now Pete's dead. She's gotten a business, all the equipment, and she can keep on trading. Plus, she's gotten rid of her annoying boss who wasn't paying her properly."

"I'm not convinced," Saracen said. "Maisie would have needed to time it perfectly to kill Pete, slip out, not be seen, and then return to work like nothing was wrong."

"She said she had an upset stomach," I said. "Maisie could have been lying to give herself more time to get it right."

Saracen grunted and scrubbed at his chin, not seeming convinced.

"Have we missed somebody?" Alice asked.

"No one else has come up on our radar," Saracen said. "Perhaps we should re-check everyone's alibi, just to be on the safe side."

We all groaned. It felt like we were taking a giant step back.

I grabbed a muffin. "Campbell won't be happy about that. We'll look like failures if we don't find the killer."

"You're right about that."

I leaped from my seat as a large hand appeared over my shoulder and grabbed a muffin. I twisted around to discover Campbell looming behind me. "I wish you wouldn't sneak up on me like that."

He grinned before biting into his muffin. "It's a part of my charm."

Alice jumped up as well. "It's so good to have you back. Has the little problem you were dealing with been sorted?"

He nodded. "Everything's in hand, Princess. The full team will be back by the end of the day."

"That's such a relief," she said. "I've missed you not being here."

Campbell slid his sunglasses out of his pocket and placed them over his eyes. "It's good to be back."

"I guess you heard everything we were saying," I said.

"All of it. I'll take over from here," Campbell said. "Standards might have slipped in my absence."

I faced him, my hands on my hips. "That's not fair. We've been working hard. I'm no expert. I did the best I could."

"But Saracen's an expert," he said.

Saracen's shoulders twitched, and a muscle in his jaw flexed, but he said nothing.

"Saracen also worked hard. He's even started talking in full sentences since I've been with him," I said. "We work well together."

"When you're not messing around with cakes," Campbell said.

"Campbell! You're being mean," Alice said. "Holly's just come second place in the food fair contest after a spectacular fail on her first cake. Plus, she figured out all the suspects in Pete's murder. You should be giving her a pat on the back."

"I'll add it to my to-do list." Campbell lifted his chin toward Saracen. "I need a debrief in private."

Saracen nodded before turning and following Campbell into the castle.

Alice huffed out a breath. "He didn't have to be so short with you. I know he must be tired from his long trip, but even so, I thought we did a good job."

I settled back on the bench and took several large bites of muffin to cool my anger.

Rupert cleared his throat before patting the back of my hand and standing. "I wish I could stay and help you figure this out, but I've got an appointment I need to get to."

Alice checked the time. She gasped and jumped to her feet. "I'm late for my art class. If Mommy hears that I've been slacking off, she won't be happy. She'll force me to spend the summer in Tuscany with her and Daddy. What a nightmare."

"I don't know how you bear such torture," I said.

She tutted at me before grabbing another muffin. "Come on, Rupert."

He looked at me. "Once again, Holly, I really am—"

"No more apologies." I held up a hand. "Second place isn't bad."

"Yes! Quite right. You're fabulous. I mean, that is to say, your cake is fabulous." He rubbed the back of his neck before nodding. "I, um, well, I'll see you around." He turned and hurried away.

I sat on the bench alone with a ton of muffins to eat and no answers to the puzzle about what had happened to Pete.

My gaze drifted to the east turret. I needed an expert to help me out with this mystery, and I knew just the eccentric, murder predicting individual to speak to.

Chapter 20

I returned to the kitchen, placed several muffins on a tray, along with a pot of tea and some cups, grabbed Meatball, and we headed to the turret to see Lady Philippa.

"And then I said, if you tell me your diamonds are paste, I'll inform you that my pearls came out of a Christmas cracker." Lady Philippa's laugh drifted toward me as we walked along the wide stone corridor to her rooms.

"And of course, I turned down the marriage proposal from the third Earl of Wells. The man's chin constantly wobbled. It was like trying to kiss a jelly."

I tapped lightly on her door. "Lady Philippa, it's Holly and Meatball. Mind if we come in?"

Footsteps strode toward the door, and she pulled it open. Lady Philippa was dressed head to toe in a bright pink velour tracksuit. "Holly! And Meatball! Of course, you're most welcome."

I stared at her clothes. "Have you been doing more online shopping?"

"Of course. Isn't it fabulous? And this is so comfortable. I'm going to get one for all the family members. It's a perfect gift idea. Would you like one?"

My mouth twisted to the side. "I'm not sure I'm made for velour."

"You'll never go back once you've tried it. Do come in. And you've brought muffins. My day keeps getting better."

I set out the muffins and poured the tea as I looked around. "Were you on the phone a moment ago?"

"No, I don't trust cellular phones."

"It's just that I heard you talking to someone."

"That was the ghosts. We have a chat most days. They get lonely floating around all on their own."

I settled in my seat and tried to hide my surprise. "Of course. That's good of you."

She settled in her own seat. "So, how did the competition go?"

"Well, after a spectacularly bad start, I came second."

Lady Philippa nodded. "An excellent effort. And you had a lot on your mind. It's a marvel you were able to fit in the contest at all."

"That's why I'm here. I'm trying to piece everything together, but none of it makes sense. When you told me about a death occurring and then Pete was killed, I thought we had it figured out. Dennis was being questioned, he has a great motive, but ..."

"Even though there was strong evidence against him, a solid motive, and opportunity, you weren't convinced?" She raised her tea cup to her lips.

"That's exactly it. He has a long-held grudge against Pete, but something's missing."

"You're over complicating things." Lady Philippa placed her cup down. "Remember what I told you before this began. Go back to the basics."

"Your prediction, you mean?"

She nodded.

"You said that pigs, wigs, and figs were involved. What does that mean? I thought it might have something to do with a meat seller at the food fair, or someone selling figs in port, or maybe dried figs, but I still can't see where the wig figures."

"That's your solution. Those three things tie this together."

"I still don't understand how."

Lady Philippa bit into a muffin. Her eyes shot open wide. "This isn't your average muffin. What's it filled with?"

I smiled. At least I'd gotten something right today. Everyone loved the muffin stack. "That's a part of my competition entry. It's a twist on a croquembouche. The muffins were filled with cream, chocolate, or caramel."

"I got chocolate. This is delicious. If I'd been judging, I'd have given you first place. What a clever idea."

"Princess Alice actually came up with the idea. It's a bit of an involved story, but that wasn't my initial entry. Princess Alice and Lord Rupert got involved, and things changed rather swiftly after that."

"Well, I'm glad they were involved if this was your offering." She licked chocolate sauce off her fingers. "Don't let your doubts hinder your intuition in this murder. You know your suspects and you have their details. One of them will fit my prediction."

I sat back in my seat as Lady Philippa told me about the half a dozen other velour tracksuits she had, all in different colors. She planned to wear one at the next ball she attended. That I wouldn't mind seeing.

Her prediction still meant nothing to me. I'd gone over it so many times and then dismissed it because the pieces wouldn't fit.

I finished my tea and muffin, collected the empty tray, and said goodbye to Lady Philippa. Maybe I needed a break, give myself time away to sort this all out. There had to be a way to figure out who killed Pete.

I should speak to Campbell. He must know what the next move would be. He'd have looked over the suspects' interviews and maybe seen a hole we'd missed. After all, he was the expert. I was nothing but an enthusiastic amateur.

I was heading back to the kitchen with Meatball when I spotted Colin walking past the castle window, a smile on his face.

He raised a hand when he saw me. I gestured him over to the kitchen, and he nodded. I met him by the kitchen door.

"Holly, I was hoping to see you before I left. I wanted to congratulate you on your second place, but you dashed off before the end of the prize giving."

"Thanks, Colin. From the smile on your face it looks like you had good news."

His grin widened. "My nut cheese got a commendation, and I've had an order from the Duchess. And to top it all, I secured three new customers. You should soon see my cheese in the local stores."

"Congratulations! I'll be sure to buy some," I said.

"Why not come and try some now?" he said. "I've been working on a nut cheese and leek pie, but I'm not sure the pastry's right. An expert opinion would be welcome. I feel like I'm on a roll and don't want to stop now."

His boyish enthusiasm was infectious. "Sure, why not?"

"My food truck's parked around the back. I was given permission to leave it there while I did business in the village. Your employers have been kind to me. I can see why you like working here."

"It has its moments, that's for sure." I walked next to Colin and waited as he unlocked the back of his food truck and stepped inside.

"I hope you don't mind, but no dogs allowed. I have to stick to the hygiene laws." Colin shrugged and nodded at Meatball.

"Of course. Meatball, sit!"

He wagged his tail and plopped his butt on the ground.

I followed Colin inside and looked around. Everything was sparkling clean and neat. A long chrome work counter was set against one side. Several delicious looking pies sat on it.

"You've got a great setup." I admired the gleaming kitchen knives secured on a magnetic knife strip.

He nodded, his chest puffing out. "I've worked hard to make this business a success. It's taken a lot of time and effort, but I'm finally getting somewhere. Here, try a slice of this." He pulled out a pie slicer and cut off a sliver of pie before handing it to me.

I took a sniff. "This has sage in it. And I'm getting a hint of something else. Maybe thyme?"

"You have a good nose," he said. "That's exactly right."

I bit through the pastry crust and into the rich savory center. Gooey warm nut cheese mingled with soft, buttery leeks. "This is a really good pie. Your cheese adds an interesting tang. It's different, but not too different, if that makes sense."

Colin beamed as he ate his own piece of pie. "That's always been my plan. Make something similar to what people are used to but different enough to catch their attention. Everyone likes a good pie, but my cheese has that extra something special."

"It really does. Is there any chance I can have the recipe?"

He smiled as he shook his head. "I can't give away my secrets. How about this one?"

We spent the next ten minutes sampling moreish, tasty pies. Colin had a knack for creating delicious combinations using his cheese and different kinds of meat and vegetables.

"I'm so impressed." I licked pie crumbs off my fingers. "Maybe I can persuade Chef Heston to have your pies in our café."

Colin's eyes widened. "That would be wonderful. If that happens, I'll have to expand. It's just the food truck and me at the moment. I was considering taking someone on part-time given all the new orders I've had following this food fair."

"You must be glad that Pete convinced you to come. It's worked out well for you."

His mouth turned down, but he nodded. "I am. Good has come out of this tragedy."

"It's just a shame the killer's still at large," I said.

Colin's eyebrows rose. "I thought they'd charged Dennis."

"They had to let him go," I said.

"That's worrying news. Pete's murder can't remain unsolved."

"I know this is a tough time for you, but focus on the positive. I imagine Pete would be happy that you're doing so well."

"He'd be slapping me on the back and telling me to buy the drinks tonight to celebrate." Colin sighed. "You're right. I have to be positive. So, how about one last pie before you go? It's a new one. I'm worried the flavors don't work."

I patted my stomach. I wouldn't be eating dinner tonight. "One more piece of pie won't hurt."

"Take a seat. I asked the chef in your kitchen to store some of my pies. I ran out of room here. I've been so full of ideas since I've gotten my new orders that I can't stop experimenting."

I chuckled as I took a seat. "I know that feeling. Sometimes, I dream about cupcakes. They get into my head and won't leave me alone until I've baked them."

"I won't be a minute." Colin hopped out of the back of the food truck.

I looked around as I waited. It was a cozy environment. It looked like the seating area could be pulled out to make a bed if needed, and the table folded away.

I stood and pulled open a drawer. Everything was squeaky clean. Colin ran a tight operation.

I looked in a cupboard and admired the top-of-the-range equipment Colin had. It seemed he was going places with his nut cheese.

I pulled open a large cabinet, expecting to find more expensive cooking supplies.

My eyes widened at the sight of two mannequin heads wearing short blond wigs.

I was just reaching for one, when the door to the food truck opened.

Colin pulled up short, a pie in his hand. "Oh! You shouldn't be looking in there." He hurried in, shutting the door behind him.

I shut the cabinet swiftly. "I'm sorry. I was just looking at your equipment. I didn't mean to pry."

Colin placed down the pie and adjusted the baseball cap on his head. "Oh, well, it's not a secret. Not really. Although I don't like to talk about it."

"Those are yours?" I gestured to the wig cabinet.

He tugged at his cap again. "I have a bit of a problem. I, um …" His words trailed off as his cheeks glowed.

"Really, you don't need to say anymore," I said. "And I must apologize. It was wrong of me to poke around."

Colin sighed. "It's the stress. It does strange things to people. And unfortunately for me, it's meant I've started to lose my hair." He pulled the hat off his head.

I'd never seen him without it on before. He had several large bald spots surrounded by thin tufts of hair.

He shoved the cap back on and grimaced. "It's not exactly attractive to look at. I don't always wear those wigs, but you won't see me out in public without either a cap or one of those. My doctor tells me I need to have better control over my nerves, but there's so much to think about when you're running a business. You have to do everything on your own. Of course that's going to be stressful."

"So long as you enjoy what you do, that's the main thing. Try not to get too stressed. You should seriously look into getting an assistant. That would remove some pressure."

"Then I'd have to worry about if I was hiring the right person, and if they were honest and reliable." Colin shook his head. "Maybe I'm better off alone. I really only trusted Pete. Look how that ended up."

I was sorry for Colin. His best friend was dead, and he was losing his hair. He deserved a break. "So, tell me all about this pie you've brought me. What's in it?"

He rubbed his hands together, looking happy to move on from his hair loss. "My speciality nut cheese, of course."

"We can't be without that," I said.

"And I've combined it with something sweet and savory. Try this and let me know what you think."

I took the piece of pie and bit into it. The pastry was the perfect crumbly combination, and I got a hit of something sweet, followed by the rich savory blast of what had to be gammon.

"This one is your best," I said. "I'm not certain what the fruit is, though. What did you use?"

"That's what I'm not sure about," Colin said. "I added a layer of nut cheese over the gammon, but combined the gammon with figs. Do you think the combination works?"

I almost choked on the pie as my gaze went to the closet containing the wigs. Oh my goodness. Pigs, wigs, and figs. Colin was the killer.

Chapter 21

I swallowed the solid lump of pie lodged in my throat as I tried to hide my panic.

"Is everything okay?" Colin asked. "Are the flavors too intense? I wondered about that. I could use a different fruit. How about gammon and dates? No, I don't think that would work. Something citrus?"

"The pie's great." I coughed and patted my chest. "Do you mind if I use your toilet?"

"Of course not. It's at the back on the right."

I dashed to the toilet, secured the door, and opened a text message to Campbell. *Hurry! Stuck in Colin's food truck. He killed Pete.* I sent it before making a show of flushing the toilet and washing my hands.

I stared at my reflection in the mirror. My dark eyes were wide and my face pale. Colin would know something was wrong.

This was too much of a coincidence. Lady Philippa's prediction had been exactly about these three things. I still couldn't figure it all out, though. Colin and Pete were supposed to be best friends. Why would he want to kill him?

Smoothing my hands over my hair, I unlocked the door and walked out, forcing a smile on my face.

Colin was sitting at the table, flicking through recipe books. He looked up as I approached. "Maybe I'm being too ambitious with the figs. I could just stick to my nut cheese and gammon."

I slid into the seat opposite him. I needed answers. "That could be tasty. Was this the combination you were trying when you worked with Pete?"

He closed the recipe book. "No, that was ground beef, nut cheese, and sage and onion. It was too traditional for my taste. I move with the times with my nut cheese, but Pete wanted something his customers would love, so I went along with it. Today's market likes to try new things. I've even come up with a few plant-based pie options."

"Are you going to finish creating the pie you'd planned with Pete? It might be a nice way to remember him."

Colin's shoulders drooped. "I don't know. I still can't believe he's gone. I expect him to wander through the door and demand to be fed. He always said my pies were the best he'd ever tasted, although he made me swear I wouldn't tell anyone that in public, otherwise his pies would look below par."

"Did you think his food was below par?"

Colin's gaze slid to the side. "It was always hit and miss. I was surprised because when you find a good supplier you stick with them. I've had a few of Pete's pies over the years. They always tasted different. I had the chicken pot pie on three occasions. Each time, it was like somebody different made them. Pete said there'd been a few changes to the recipe and not to worry about it. But now and again, the quality wasn't good. I never said anything. It was his business, and he was doing well."

"It sounds like you did most things with Pete," I said.

"That's what best friends are for," Colin said.

"Were you planning on taking a holiday together?"

His eyes narrowed. "No, we've never been away together. Why do you ask?"

"I saw Pete's vacation plans on his laptop. He was looking at flights to Australia." That was technically true. I didn't need to tell Colin that I'd only seen those plans after Pete had been killed.

Colin's head lowered. "He never mentioned a vacation to me."

"Perhaps he was going with a girlfriend."

"No, no vacation and no girlfriend." His hands flexed around the recipe book.

"If not a vacation, was he taking some time out? Maybe doing some traveling."

"No." Colin tapped his fingers on the table.

I nodded slowly. "He wasn't relocating to Australia, was he?"

His lips pursed. "No! It was all talk. He was never serious when he discussed selling up. Pete only mentioned it when he was drunk."

My eyebrows shot up. "Pete was leaving for good? He wanted to emigrate?"

Colin tipped his head back and stared at the ceiling for a second. "He shouldn't have kept it a secret. I couldn't believe it when I heard him making plans. He was negotiating to get a cheap deal on the phone. He managed to charm the agent into giving him ten percent off the price."

"When did you hear him do that?" I tried not to sound eager, but this could be the missing piece I was looking for.

Colin was quiet for several seconds. "I ... don't remember."

I discreetly pulled out my phone and checked it. There was no response from Campbell. I was on my own when it came to squeezing a confession out of Colin.

My gaze ran over him. He didn't look like a strong man and was only a few inches taller than me. I might be able to take him, but there were lots of sharp objects in this food truck. I needed to be careful, or I'd end up just like Pete.

"It must have been hard on you when you learned Pete was leaving, especially since you were so close. Good friends are hard to find."

"I wish he'd just told me what he was doing," Colin said. "We could have gone together. I'm not a fan of the sun, but I could have put up with it. I'm sure Australians would love my nut cheese. Pete never mentioned it, though. Now, it's too late. He won't be going anywhere."

"Did you hear Pete talking about his travel plans when he was at the food fair?" I asked.

Colin looked away, and his jaw wobbled. "It doesn't matter now. Pete's gone. He can never go to Australia and leave me on my own."

My heart thudded like I'd just run a marathon. I leaned closer. "Colin, did you confront Pete? You must have been angry that he didn't tell you his plans. They didn't include you. You must have hated that."

He slid the recipe book away and stood before pacing the length of the food truck. "Pete was my best friend. We told each other everything. He was the only person who ever stood up for me. Everyone teased me about my cheese. I knew I was onto something good, and Pete agreed with me. He pushed me when no one else thought I stood a chance."

"Which is why it must have been difficult when you learned he was no longer going to be around. He was your support system, and he was ripping it out from under your feet."

Colin shook his head as the pacing increased. "We were working on a pie together. He couldn't just leave. Pete was booking a flight that left in two weeks' time."

"And you got angry about that, didn't you," I said quietly. "You felt let down."

Colin scrubbed at his face. "Of course. Pete was supposed to be my friend, but was just the same as everybody else. He didn't like me. He simply saw me as a business opportunity. He recognized that I'd found a profitable niche and wanted in. He decided we could use his nasty pies, add my cheese, and we'd have a whole new market open to us."

"Did he tell you that?"

"He didn't have to. The fact he was going to walk away was proof enough that I wasn't really his friend. I was convenient and offered him something. A way to make more money so he could fund his new life in the sun. Once he stepped on that plane, I'd have never heard from him again."

"Did you see his laptop with his plans on? Pete had been looking into flights while he was working that day."

Colin glared at me. "You know a lot about this. Were you going with him?"

"No! But I understand that you'd have been furious after hearing that conversation and seeing the information." I'd always thought this murder was personal and not some opportunistic theft gone wrong.

Colin dropped his head into his hands and groaned. "I've always been alone. Most of my life I've been desperately lonely. It changed when Pete showed up. He was like this ball of energy. He made me believe in myself. Then he turned his back on me. He showed me that I didn't matter. I never mattered to him. I never matter to anyone."

"I'm sure there are people who care for you," I said.

"Who? My parents are dead. I'm an only child. I never had any friends at school. Then I started making my nut cheese, and all I got was ridiculed. I was on the verge of giving up when Pete stepped in and suggested I had a good product." He swallowed loudly. "He turned out to be the biggest traitor of them all."

"Why did you put Pete's laptop in Dennis's food truck?" I asked.

Colin's head jerked back, but then he shrugged. "Why not? He's a hateful man who bullied me. He was always taunting me. He said my cheese tastes like old socks that had been left out in the sun. As you've just proven that's not true. Unless you were lying too?"

I raised my hands quickly. "Absolutely not. You have a great product. But you shouldn't have framed Dennis."

"The world would be a better place with him behind bars. Dennis is a bully, and he hated Pete."

I summoned every ounce of courage. "He may have hated Pete, but you killed him."

Colin stared at me, his right eye twitching and his body shaking. "It was an accident. I wasn't in my right mind. I overheard him on the phone, and I saw red. I've never felt rage like it."

"Where were you when you heard his conversation?"

"Outside the marquee. I was walking around, working off the aches in my calf muscles from standing all day. I heard Pete's voice and stopped to listen. I couldn't believe it. I checked no one was watching and crept under the side of the marquee. Pete had his back to me. He sounded so smug and sure of himself. Then I saw the open laptop which confirmed my fears. He was booking a one-way ticket to Australia."

"That's when you grabbed the pie slicer and killed him?"

"I couldn't let him get away with it. Pete used me and was throwing me away like a piece of trash." Colin's gaze met mine, and his eyes filled with tears before they hardened. "I wish you hadn't come here, Holly. I genuinely like you."

My throat tightened as I stood slowly. "And I like you, Colin. But what you did was wrong. You have to tell the police."

"No! What I have to do is leave. No one suspects me, other than you. I still can't figure out how you put it all together."

I glanced at the closed cabinet containing the wigs. "Let's just say I had a little help."

Colin blocked the door as I went to move. It was my only way out. "I'll make this easy on you. It doesn't have to hurt, but I can't let you leave. You'll tell that security guy who's been sniffing around what I've told you. I don't hold up well under pressure." He pulled off his cap and scratched his balding head.

Scuffling came from the closed truck door. Meatball must have sensed I was in trouble and was trying to get in to help.

"You're not a cold-blooded killer." My voice wobbled. "You acted out of character because of your … difficult situation. The police will understand that, but they won't be lenient if you kill me too."

"If they cross-examine me, I'll break, just like I did with you. Everyone's right when they say I'm a weak man. I was an idiot to let my guard down and allow someone in. Look where it's gotten me." He reached for a crumb covered knife.

I shook my head, my insides wobbling and my brain screaming at me to run. But there was nowhere to go. Colin had me trapped.

His hand shook as he held out the knife. "Close your eyes, Holly."

"You're not thinking clearly. We'll go and talk to the police together. They'll understand that there are mitigating circumstances. Pete lied to you. He lied to a lot of people."

"No! You don't get to say a bad word about him. Even after his betrayal, he's still my best friend. My only friend. You don't insult him."

"But you do? You killed him. That's the biggest insult you can give to a person."

Meatball barked loudly from outside.

Colin's gaze hardened. "That's enough. This ends now."

I grabbed the gammon and fig pie as Colin lunged at me, dodging to the left to avoid the knife strike as I slammed the pie, china plate and all, straight into his face.

There was a horrible crunching noise. Colin squealed as blood gushed from his nose. He staggered back, dropping the knife.

The door to the food truck was yanked open. Campbell charged in, a blur of contained fury and muscle.

Meatball was right behind him, barking loudly.

I pointed a shaking finger at Colin. "Here's your killer."

Chapter 22

The hill I cycled up felt particularly steep this afternoon. I reached the top and pulled up, petting Meatball on the head as I looked out over the stunning vista that surrounded Audley St. Mary. My home. Beautiful, and safe once again.

I cocked my head as the rumble of trucks drew near. It was the remaining trucks from the food fair leaving the village.

I lifted a hand and waved them goodbye as they trundled past.

Everything at the castle was back to normal. The marquees were being dismantled and the last of the vendors were gone.

I might not have won the cake competition, but I'd helped to solve a murder and catch a killer. That felt like success to me.

I was about to freewheel down the hill, when a sleek black limousine pulled up beside me. The window rolled down and Lady Philippa stared out at me.

"Holly! May we offer you a lift?" She rested a manicured, ring-covered hand on the door.

"Goodness! This is the first time I've seen you out of the castle," I said. "Is this a special occasion?"

"It is." Alice's head appeared. "We're going out for lunch."

Rupert's head poked past Lady Philippa's shoulder, and he gave me a cheery wave.

"I convinced them to let me out of my prison for the afternoon," Lady Philippa said in a conspiratorial whisper.

I chuckled. "Good for you."

An angry yipping came from inside the limousine.

"And you're taking Horatio too," I said.

"Not that he appreciates it, the lazy old hound," Lady Philippa said. "He'd much rather sleep on my bed and get his fur everywhere."

Meatball barked in response to Horatio's yapping, which only made him worse.

"We're going to see Olivia Brown," Lady Philippa said. "After our conversation the other day, I thought it might be nice to mend a few bridges. We used to have a laugh when we were younger. If I apologize for my comments, we might be able to have some fun together again."

I smiled brightly. "That's a perfect idea. I expect you'll have a great time."

"You must come with us," Alice said. "The whole village is talking about what happened in the food truck with Colin."

"I'd never have figured him as the killer," Rupert said.

"And that's why he made the perfect killer," I said. "He went almost unnoticed." It seemed like that was the rather sad story of Colin Cheeseman's whole life.

It had been two days since I'd narrowly escaped being killed by Colin. Campbell had frogmarched him away from the food truck, and he'd been charged after confessing to Pete's murder.

Since then, I'd kept a low profile. Mainly because I knew Audley St. Mary would be alive with gossip about the incident, but almost getting stabbed was a shock to the system. I'd needed some down time to recover.

"The worm definitely turned in this case," Lady Philippa said. "I always say that you need to watch the quiet ones. They're only quiet because they have dark thoughts in their head that they're focused on. Although I did get to try his nut cheese. It was tasty. It's a shame there won't be any coming to the castle."

"Even though he did a terrible thing," I said, "I feel sorry for him. Colin was mistreated by a lot of people. He was never taken seriously. He worked hard on something he believed in."

"That doesn't give him an excuse to stab someone in the back with a pie slicer," Alice said. "You're too kind-hearted, Holly."

"I'm just glad my pigs, wigs, and figs solved it for you." Lady Philippa winked at me.

"What's all this?" Rupert asked.

"Oh, nothing important," I said.

"Please come with us," Alice said. "There's plenty of room in the limo. You can put the bike in the trunk. Granny will keep hold of Horatio so he can't be mean to Meatball. Olivia would love to have a first-hand account of how you were inches from death and saved the day by breaking Colin's nose with his own pie."

I winced. I had hit him hard. His face was so swollen when he'd been taken away that he was almost unrecognizable.

I looked to the horizon, where the castle proudly stood. "I should get back to the kitchen. Chef Heston has me on double shifts. I have a mountain of vegetables to peel." Despite coming second in the cake competition, Chef Heston hadn't budged on the deal we'd made. I was peeling, scrubbing, and working extra hard in the kitchen. Although I had noticed a little bonus in my wage packet yesterday, so maybe he wasn't quite as mean as he liked to make out he was.

"I can order you to do this," Alice said. "You know that if anyone disobeys my orders, they end up in the tower. And the really naughty ones—"

"I know, they end up having their heads chopped off." I laughed. "With an offer like that, how can I refuse?"

The limo driver climbed out, and I lifted Meatball out of his basket before the bike was slid into the trunk.

The front passenger door opened, and I stepped back as Campbell appeared. I hadn't seen him since he'd interviewed me and taken Colin away.

"A word, Holly." He led me a short distance from the limo.

I grimaced. I was no doubt about to be reprimanded for interfering in yet another investigation. "Just one word?"

The side of his mouth quirked up. "I want to commend you on your work. Colin's confession stands up. Although you really didn't need to give our killer a broken nose."

"Broken nose! Oh! I didn't realize it was broken. I was only trying to stop him from killing me."

"I'm glad you did. You did an excellent job," he said. "When I received your text, I wasn't sure if it was a joke. Fortunately for you, I had some spare time and came to investigate."

"Lucky me," I said.

"And thanks to your noisy dog, I knew exactly which truck was Colin's."

"He is a wonder dog." I cuddled Meatball tighter. He'd been there when I needed him, helping to keep me safe.

Campbell drew in a long breath. "Since it appears you want to keep poking around in dangerous investigations, it's time you had training. You need to be prepared the next time you take on a killer one-on-one when you're unarmed and in a confined space."

I shook my head. "Oh, no. There's not going to be a next time. I'm all done with solving murders."

"I recall that you said that the last time you confronted a killer," Campbell said.

I grinned. "I mean, there's a certain satisfaction in finding out who did it. And I didn't mean to get trapped in the food truck with Colin. He enticed me with his pies, then everything clicked into place."

"You need to be more careful about going off with strange men."

"Duly noted. Do you consider yourself to be a strange man?"

"One of the strangest." He rapped his knuckles on my cycle helmet and then petted Meatball. "If I tell you to keep away from future investigations, will you?"

"I will, but there are conditions attached to that. I mean, if I'm directly implicated in the murder and you consider me a suspect, I'll have to prove my innocence. And if someone's killed at an event I'm involved with, and I discover the body, then I'm going to want to find out what happened. And—"

"Enough! Being nosy is in your nature. I don't think there's anything I can do about that."

"You should be glad I'm nosy," I said. "But I prefer the term naturally curious. If it wasn't for my natural curiosity, you may never have discovered what Colin did."

Campbell glowered at me. "One more thing. If you discover that a member of my team is keeping a secret, you tell me immediately."

I bit my lip. "Who are we talking about?"

"You know who. Saracen's told me everything."

"And he still has a job?"

He nodded. "For now."

"You can't fire him. For some weird reason, he loves working for you."

Campbell snorted a laugh. "Everyone loves me. Get in the car, Holly Holmes."

I suppressed laughter as I walked back to the limo. Campbell opened the door for me, and I slid in next to Lady Philippa, who gave my knee a squeeze.

"Is everything good? Campbell not being a problem?"

I looked around in the car full of wonderful, quirky oddballs who I considered my extended family. "No problem. Everything's perfect."

"It will be when we get to Olivia's cottage," Alice said. "I ordered two dozen of your chocolate swirl cupcakes to have as a dessert."

"Then it really will be a good lunch." I sat back and listened to them chatter among themselves. I'd been embraced by this warm, eclectic family, and my heart thudded with happiness.

This last week had been a whirlwind of cakes, catastrophe, and chaos. As dazed as I was by it all, I wouldn't have it any other way. This felt like a real win.

I had wonderful friends, a job I loved, and my best furry friend snuggled on my knee.

Everything was sweetly perfect in Audley St. Mary's once again.

About Author

K.E. O'Connor (Karen) is a cozy mystery author living in the beautiful British countryside. She loves all things mystery, animals, and cake (these often feature in her books.)

When she's not writing about mysteries, murder, and treats, she volunteers at a local animal sanctuary, reads a ton of books, binge watches mystery series on TV, and dreams about living somewhere warmer.

To stay in touch with the fun, clean mysteries, where the killer always gets their just desserts:

Newsletter: www.subscribepage.com/cozymysteries
Website: www.keoconnor.com/writing
Facebook: www.facebook.com/keoconnorauthor

Also By

Enjoy the complete Holly Holmes cozy culinary mysteries in paperback or e-book.

Cream Caramel and Murder

Chocolate Swirls and Murder

Vanilla Whip and Murder

Cherry Cream and Murder

Blueberry Blast and Murder

Mocha Cream and Murder

Lemon Drizzle and Murder

Maple Glaze and Murder

Mint Frosting and Murder

Read on for a peek at book three in the series - Vanilla Whip and Murder!

Chapter 1

"One more big push and we can freewheel down the next hill, Meatball."

"Woof woof." My adorable corgi cross poked his tongue out, and his stubby tail wagged as the wind blew his ears back.

I sucked in a deep breath as the last hill in Audley St. Mary confronted me. I was tired from a morning of cake deliveries around the pretty village. It seemed like everyone couldn't get enough of the delicious treats we made at Audley Castle.

A car rumbled up behind me before slowing, and the horn was tooted.

I inched to the edge of the road. It was a narrow lane, so it made it tricky for cars to pass me safely.

The horn tooted again, several times.

I lifted my right hand off the handlebar and gestured for them to drive around me.

The car maneuvered next to me and the window slid down. Cecilia Montgomery smiled at me. "Busy day, Holly?"

"It's always busy at the castle, Cecilia. How's the dress shop going?"

"I can't complain. I had Princess Alice in just last week. She bought half of my stock."

"She does love to shop," I said.

"You won't hear me complaining about that. Have a nice day." Cecilia tooted her horn again before zooming off in her sporty black two-seater. The couture business was clearly doing well for her.

I gave Meatball a quick tickle under his furry brown chin before digging in and making it to the crest of the hill, trying hard not to wish for a car just like Cecilia's. Cars cost money, and my work bike was a free and easy way to keep fit.

And with all the cycling I'd done today on my delivery round, I more than deserved the strawberry cream pie nestled in the bike basket. It was tucked in a box to keep it away from Meatball.

At my last delivery, Mr. Johnson had not only given me a tip but also one of my own cakes. I was planning on putting my feet up for five minutes and enjoying it with a big mug of tea before I got on with the baking that needed doing in the Audley Castle kitchen.

Loud dance music pounded from a vehicle approaching behind me at speed. I hugged the curb and concentrated on keeping the wheels of the bike straight to give the vehicle enough room to pass me.

A horn blasted and there was a screech of tires. My back wheel was bumped.

I gasped and clutched the handlebars. You have got to be kidding me? Someone was trying to run me off the road.

"Woof!" Meatball's eyes narrowed, and he growled.

"It's okay. It's just someone who needs to go back to driver's school."

My back wheel was nudged again. That time, it was deliberate.

"Get off the road, you idiot!" A shiny red sports car screeched around me, the music blaring and the windows down. There was a flash of long dark hair, and then it was gone.

"I'm the idiot?" I tried to get control of the bike, but the front wheel hit a hole in the road, and I lurched sideways.

I reached out and caught Meatball to keep him safe as the bike pitched over.

I crashed to the ground, Meatball protected by my arms forming a shield around him. A pedal whacked my shin as I hit the muddy ground with a bone jarring thump.

I blinked several times, my heart thundering, and my breath coming out in panicked gasps. "That crazy driver could have killed us."

Meatball licked the palm of my hand and whined.

"Are you okay, boy?" I used my free hand to lift the heavy frame of the bike off me and winced as I pulled my leg out from underneath it. Nothing felt broken, but there was a gash on my shin.

Once I was free from under the bike, I scooped Meatball up and checked him over. As usual, he wore his cycling helmet and had been cushioned from the fall by my arms and his blanket.

I cuddled him to me as I twisted my ankles in different directions. Nothing felt strained, but the cuts on my legs stung and the skin felt hot.

I groaned as I checked the bike. The front wheel had buckled when I'd hit the hole.

This wouldn't be the first time I'd damaged the castle's delivery bike. My boss, Chef Heston, would be less than impressed. He'd no doubt take the repairs for the bike out of my wages. But this wasn't my fault. That terrible driver had almost killed me, and he hadn't even slowed down to make sure I was okay. He must have seen me fall off the bike.

A driver in a sleek soft top black Audi cruised past. The brake lights flashed on before the car reversed and stopped beside me. The passenger side window slid down.

A guy with brilliant blue eyes and a hint of dark stubble on his chin leaned over and peered down at me. He looked vaguely familiar. "What are you doing down there?"

"Thanking my lucky stars that I wasn't killed by some idiot in a sports car who doesn't know how to drive," I said. "He just ran me off the road. He hit my bike with his car, twice. He didn't even stop after I fell."

The guy rested a hand on the open window shelf, and I saw a flash of green and black tattoo swirls lacing up his forearm.

I placed Meatball on the ground and stood slowly, my left leg protesting as I did so.

"Did you get his license plate?" the guy asked. "You can always report him to the police."

"No, I was too busy trying not to fall off my bike."

"You didn't do a good job of that." A smirk crossed his face.

"You think!" I wasn't usually this sharp with people, but my heart still raced from the close call. "Hey, are you going to Audley Castle? I won't be able to ride my bike back. I could do with a lift."

He was silent for a long second. "The castle? Why are you going there?"

"I work there," I said.

"Are you a cleaner or something?"

"No! What makes you say that?"

"I definitely didn't figure you for a member of the Audley family." He chuckled as his gaze ran over me.

"Maybe I decided not to wear my tiara today when I came out on a ride. For all you know, you could be speaking to Princess Alice Audley."

He tipped his head back and roared with laughter. "You're not her. I've seen plenty of pictures of Princess Alice. You're the complete opposite of her. She's blonde, curvy, and cute. You're ..." He waved a hand at me.

I bristled at his implied insult. I may not have curves to die for, but I was happy with the way I looked. "Even so, I could be a cousin or a relative of the family."

"But are you?"

I huffed out a breath. "No! But I am in need of help after almost being killed. Surely you can fit my bike in the back of your car. Audley Castle isn't far from here."

He checked his watch and shook his head. "No can do. I'm late for an appointment. Besides, I'm not going that way. Nothing's broken, is it?"

"That's hardly the point. I could be in shock. I may have a concussion. I'm a damsel in distress."

"You're also a damsel wearing an enormous cycling helmet who's quite happy to stand here and argue with me. That suggests your head is fine. You can find your own way to the castle." He roared the engine as the window slid up, and he zoomed off.

My mouth dropped open. So much for chivalry.

Meatball whined, and I turned to see him sniffing the squashed cake box underneath the bike.

I gently eased the bike off the box. It was squashed flat. My delicious treat was ruined, along with the rest of my day, all thanks to my encounter with unhelpful men driving cars that probably cost ten years of my salary.

I righted the bike and checked the front wheel. It was too crooked to ride.

I reached into my back pocket where my phone usually was. Just perfect. I must have left it back in my apartment. I'd been running late that morning, and it had been a mad dash to get to the kitchen in time.

"It looks like we have to help ourselves, Meatball." I scooped him up, kissed him on the head, and placed him back in the basket. "At least I have you. You'll never let me down."

"Woof woof." He rested his front paws on the edge of the basket as I slowly pushed the damaged bike toward the castle. It was only about a mile away, but with my sore leg, it felt a lot farther.

"If I ever see that idiot driver again, we're having words. Why is it always the people who drive the posh sports cars who have terrible manners and are awful drivers?" That wasn't always true, but I was too angry to be rational. "If I was in charge, I'd make anyone who drove a sports car have extra driving lessons so they knew how to handle something so powerful."

"Woof woof." Meatball heartily agreed as he surveyed the beautiful countryside I limped past.

At least the weather was on our side. It was a glorious sunny day, and white clouds scudded across a brilliant blue sky. Birds sung in the treetops, and by the time I'd reached the gates of Audley Castle, my bad mood had faded. Despite losing my cake, twisting my bike wheel, and having a scratched-up leg, there was always something positive to focus upon.

"Good gracious, what happened to you?" Lord Rupert Audley raced toward me as I walked along the gravel driveway toward the entrance to the kitchen.

"I met someone who doesn't know how to drive." I happily let him take the bike off me.

Rupert pushed his messy blond hair out of his eyes, and his gaze ran over me. "You haven't been hurt, have you?"

"A few cuts on my leg, but nothing serious," I said. "The bike definitely came off worse."

"Let's get this bike back to the shed and get you patched up," he said. "Do you need to see the doctor? You didn't hit your head?"

I rapped my knuckles on my helmet. "No. I was shocked when it happened, but I'll be fine."

"Your pants are torn," Rupert said. "And you've cut your knee."

"The bike fell on me, and I hit some stones when I landed," I said. "It's just a surface wound."

"You should take the rest of the day off," he said. "I can look after you. It'll be my pleasure to make sure the finest baker in the castle is safe and well. We don't want you out of action and depriving the world of your desserts."

I grinned. After my encounter with two unpleasant men, it was nice to meet a genuinely sweet person. Rupert always had a way of making me feel better.

"There's no need. And I've still got work to do in the kitchen before I can finish for the day."

"I'm sure Chef Heston won't mind if you need the afternoon off," he said. "Maybe I could suggest it to him."

"No! Chef Heston thinks I curry favor with you so I don't have to work so hard."

"I don't believe you'd ever do that. I've never seen anyone work as hard as you do," Rupert said.

I did work hard, but that was because I loved what I did. I always got such satisfaction from making delicious treats and cakes to sell to people. I felt lucky to work in Audley Castle and be surrounded by all this finery every day.

A loud squeal pierced my ears, and I winced as I stepped back.

A woman with long blonde hair raced toward Rupert and engulfed him in an enormous hug. "I've been wondering where you were." She planted a kiss on his cheek.

From her high forehead, bright blue eyes, and heart-shaped face, she had to be one of the Duke and Duchess's daughters.

"Caroline! I didn't know you'd arrived." Rupert scooped Meatball out and placed him on the ground before setting the bike down and hugging her back. "You look as striking as ever."

"And you look as messy as ever." She ruffled his hair. "Are you sure there aren't birds nesting up there?"

He chuckled as he glanced at me. His gaze went over Caroline's shoulder to the woman standing just behind her. She was shorter and thinner and her hair was pale brown.

"Henrietta, I'm glad you could make it," he said.

She nodded and lifted her cheek as he went over to kiss her. "I didn't have much choice."

"Don't be a spoilsport," Caroline said. "Who doesn't love a party?"

Henrietta raised her hand.

Caroline tutted and shook her head. "You're such a party pooper."

"I haven't seen you at the castle for such a long time," Rupert said.

"I've been too busy traveling to visit," Caroline said.

"More like wasting her trust fund," Henrietta muttered.

I felt the urge to make a discreet exit. When I was around Rupert and Alice, it was easy to forget that they were part of an ancient noble family, with royal connections. They always made me feel so welcome and at ease.

Rupert turned to me and extended a hand, as if sensing my discomfort. "This is Holly Holmes. She's the most exquisite baker you will ever discover. She works in our kitchens. We were extremely lucky to get her."

I nodded at both women. "It's nice to meet you."

"These are my cousins, Caroline and Henrietta Audley," Rupert said.

Just as I'd figured, two of the Duke and Duchess's daughters. They had four daughters, Caroline, Henrietta,

Diana, and Mary.

"I look forward to trying your cakes." Caroline tilted her head. "Actually, I've heard about them before. Rupert's always going on about the delicious treats he gets from the kitchen. I always get hungry when he talks about them. Is that your work?"

"Sometimes," I said. "Desserts are my speciality."

"She really is excellent," Rupert said.

"If that's the case, I shall steal her for our kitchen," Caroline said. "Rupert always lets me have whatever I want."

"Holly will never leave us," Rupert said, shooting me a shy look. "I expect you're involved with the anniversary party food. It won't be the same without your tempting treats."

I shook my head. "Chef Heston is leading on that, and there's an outside team coming in to make the preparations."

"Of course. Only the best for our sister." Caroline rolled her eyes. "Honestly, the amount of money they spent on that wedding; now they're doing it all again simply for a boring anniversary."

"They've been married five years," Rupert said. "That's something to celebrate."

Caroline sighed. "I guess so. Diana even had the cheek to issue a gift list. She's not getting anything from me. Not until she returns my favorite cashmere that she borrowed and never gave back. That can be her gift. Although I'm not sure it will suit her husband."

"It should be a fun party," Rupert said. "It's nice to get everyone back together."

"Not everybody's here," Henrietta said quietly, her gaze on the ground.

"Yes! Silly Mary made some excuse about traveling. She sent her apologies," Caroline said. "I'm glad she's not here. My sister's sour face would spoil the party. And if she did come, she'd only say something rude and upset everyone."

Rupert chuckled and rubbed the back of his neck. "She's not that bad. Mary simply likes to speak her mind."

"She likes saying outrageous things to annoy people and cause a scandal," Caroline said. "I don't know why she can't just let her hair down and enjoy herself."

"Like you, you mean," Henrietta said. "Your hair is always down."

Caroline jabbed a finger at her. "Don't you start. You're not much better than Mary. I bet you bring a book to the party. If I see you sneaking out to the library, I'm dragging you back and forcing you to dance. And I'm going to make sure you wear something nice."

"I always wear nice things." Henrietta smoothed her hands down her plain navy, knee-length dress.

"I'm going to do your hair and makeup and make you wear something low-cut. This is a proper party," Caroline said.

Henrietta simply shook her head and looked toward the castle.

"We must go." Caroline pressed another kiss to Rupert's cheek. "I need to catch up with Mommy and Daddy and tell them all my news. And if I have to sort out Henrietta's terrible hair, I need all the time I can get. Maybe we should dye it."

"You're not touching my hair," Henrietta said.

"We'll see about that." Caroline grabbed Henrietta's arm.

"I'll see you both later for dinner," Rupert said.

"Of course. We've got so much to catch up on, and I want to hear everything about the party plans. I can't wait." Caroline hurried away with Henrietta.

Rupert returned to my side, picked up the bike, and we walked over to the sheds. "That's the first time you've met my cousins, isn't it?"

I nodded. "I can see the family resemblance."

"They're great fun," he said. "As you may have noticed, Caroline's the life and soul of the party. Henrietta, not so much, but I like her quiet ways."

"They both seem very nice," I said. I stopped dead and my eyes widened. Parked around the side of the castle was the red sports car that had run me off the road.

"Is something wrong?" Rupert asked.

Meatball growled at the car before running over to sniff it.

"Who does that car belong to?" I asked.

"Oh! I think that's Blaine's car. He's a friend of Percy's, Diana's husband. I suspect he'll be coming to the party tomorrow night. He must have gotten here early."

My gaze narrowed, and I pressed my lips together. So, the idiot who had almost killed me was going to be at this party. If I had a mind to, I might doctor his food as revenge. Maybe some chocolate laxatives in his dessert would teach him a lesson.

I shook my head. I wasn't that vindictive, but it was tempting.

"You don't like the car?" Rupert asked when I didn't respond.

"Oh! Sorry, my mind was elsewhere. It's a great car. A bit flashy for my taste, though." I gave it one more glare, giving a nod of satisfaction when Meatball peed up a wheel.

"Are you sure you're okay to work?" Rupert placed the damaged bike in the shed and shut the door.

"Of course. It takes a lot to keep me out of the kitchen. I must go. Thanks for helping me with the bike." We said our goodbyes, and I limped away.

I settled Meatball into his kennel outside the kitchen and removed his helmet, taking mine off as well, before heading into the kitchen.

I shrugged off my jacket, hung up the cycling helmets, and walked through to wash up before beginning a relaxing afternoon of baking.

My jaw dropped, and I stopped walking.

Standing in the center of the kitchen, with a smug look on his face, was the tattooed man who'd refused to help me.

Vanilla Whip and Murder is available to buy in paperback or e-book format.

ISBN: 978-1-9163573-2-7

Here's one more treat. Enjoy this delicious recipe for tempting chocolate swirl cake. Meatball and Lord Rupert approved!

Recipe – Tempting Chocolate Swirl Cake

Prep time: 20 minutes **Cook time:** 40 minutes

Recipe can be made dairy and egg-free. Substitute milk for a plant/nut alternative, use dairy-free spread, and mix 3 tbsp flaxseed with 1 tbsp water to create one flax 'egg' as a binding agent (this recipe requires 12 tbsp flaxseed to substitute the 4 eggs.)

INGREDIENTS
1 cup (227g) unsalted butter, softened
1 cup (227g) caster sugar
4 medium free-range eggs
1 cup (227g) self-raising flour, plus extra for dusting
1 tsp vanilla extract
100ml milk, plus 1 tbsp extra
3 tbsp cocoa powder
1 tbsp chocolate sprinkles, to decorate

For the ganache:
1 tbsp golden syrup
1/4 cup (57g) caster sugar
3/4 cup (96g) dark chocolate, broken up

INSTRUCTIONS

1. Preheat the oven to 350F (180°C), fan oven 320F (160°C)

2. Beat the butter with the sugar until light and creamy. Add the eggs, one at a time, mixing well.

3. Mix in the flour, vanilla and 100ml milk until smooth.

4. Spoon half the mixture into another bowl and stir in the cocoa and 1 tablespoon milk.

5. Grease a 20cm cake tin and dust with flour. Place alternate spoonfuls of each mixture into the cake tin. Drag through a skewer to create a marbled effect.

6. Bake for 30 minutes, then cover with foil and bake for a further 10 minutes, or until a skewer inserted comes out clean. Leave to cool for 10 minutes.

7. For the ganache, heat the syrup, sugar, and 2 tablespoons of water in a pan. Bring to the boil, then remove from the heat. Add the chocolate. Leave to melt, then stir until glossy. Spread on the cake and top with sprinkles.

Cook's tip: if you don't have chocolate sprinkles, top with chopped nuts or chocolate shavings.

Cook's tip two: Buy readymade ganache. I like Cadbury icing, but any store bought will work.